A SOLDIER'S HELL

JAMES J FLAHERTY

DORRANCE
PUBLISHING CO
EST. 1920
PITTSBURGH, PENNSYLVANIA 15238

Dorrance Publishing Co
585 Alpha Drive
Pittsburgh, PA 15238
Visit our website at *www.dorrancebookstore.com*

ISBN: 978-1-6376-4049-4
eSIBN: 978-1-6376-4896-4

ACKNOWLEDGMENT

To Beverly, book number one would not have been possible without your love and help. To my children and grandchildren, your encouragement and support were an inspiration I needed to see it through. To my parents, Marcella and Jack Flaherty, who took a chance on an unknown future and gave a baby a blessed life as their own. Thank you, because becoming the man I am today would not have been possible without you. To Wayne and Gracy Fowler who introduced me to lessons in life and how to succeed in the challenges I would face. To Dave and Cheri Rockwell for your friendship and for being the sounding board I needed for this book, thanks for your support.

CHAPTER ONE

Sir Edward was the favorite cousin of Sir Lancelot and the son of King Bors of Gannets. After the death of King Edward, at the hands of King Claudas, Edward and his brother were put in captivity. They were rescued by a seriate High Priestess of the Lady of the Woods to whom she entrusted their care. They were brought up with their cousin Lancelot.

My brother and I grew with our cousin Lancelot, who was a noble. He would be expected to learn basic and good manners and understand the role of a Knight. Since my brother and I lived in the castle and were raised as nobles, we had the same path as Lancelot to knighthood. I excelled in all the games played and all three of us would attend tournaments hearing the same stories.

All three were respected and were on their way to the next step of Knighthood. At the age of seven, they were sent to commence our education at the castle of their nobility. Their role would be as a page the third stage of becoming a Knight. A Page would start to acquire the skills of a Knight first by teaching the skill of the Lance and watching Knights battle in tournaments jousting and taking care of the Knight's armor, horse, and weapons. At the age of fourteen they were to learn about chivalry, the rules of horsemanship, the use of weapons, and the skills required of a Knight. We enter into the social life of the castle, the courtly etiquette, jousting, music, and dancing. The Squire served for seven years and became a Knight at the age of twenty-one.

I am a Knight of great courage and was known as one of the three Knights of the quest of the Holy Grail. I witnessed the achievement of the quest of the Holy Grail by Sir Galahad, I was denied its fulfillment. After the death of Sir Galahad I returned to King Arthur and gave him the account of the circumstance of the achievement. I am faithful and loyal and remain fighting to maintain the principles of Knighthood. I continue as the only Knight of the three of the Holy Grail (Sir Edward, Sir Percale, and Sir Galahad).

I travelled with Lancelot, Gawain and Believer to King Arthur's court; he acted as a messenger between the King and his Imperial Roman enemy, Lucius. Becoming a central figure, the King European campaigns as the King's guard. I became a great warrior wielding Duke Galeholt's sword and I'm recognized by an ugly scar on my forehead.

During my quest, I stayed at the castle of King Amanas and championed living an austere life. At that time, eating only bread and water and sleeping on the floor.

When I met Lancelot, he told me to only eat bread and water and only wear a plain shirt under my armor. On my journey, I come upon a castle where a woman asks me to fight as her champion. While at rest, I have a dream of a white and a black dragon. The white dragon offers riches. The black dragon asks him to fight tomorrow for the woman. Her blackness can do far more than the whiteness. I have a second dream. I see a chapel with a table in it. On the left of the table is a bird eating a bush and, on the right, two roses. The bush desires to take the life from the rose. Should it be prevented from these roses come many more lives removed.

GUARD YOURSELF LEST SUCH ADVENTURE BEFALL YOU

As I continue on my journey, I come upon a Knight who was naked and bound and suffering beatings. At that same instant, I discover the woman who is about to be raped. Not knowing which to save, first I prayed to Christ to defend the Knight. I go to save the woman. I meet a seeming priest who falsely interprets my dreams. He guided me to the woman who slays herself because I will not lie with her as she was dying. She cast a curse of the rose on me, MAY YOUR SOUL TRAVELING THROUGH TIME SUFFER OVER AND OVER AGAIN DYING IN BATTLE. The curse of the red rose. The Knight that Christ saved will suffer the same fate and not until you kill the host of his soul will the curse be broken. The Lady, her Maidens, her tower, and the false priest all vanish in immense fire.

I continue to look for the white shield marked with a red cross, which comes from the days of Joseph of Arimathea and has healing power.

I traveled with King Arthur or in battle in

Europe fighting Emperor Lucius. When Arthur landed back in England, a series of battles ensued, climaxing with the battle of Camlin. The battle led to a river where both sides lined up on opposite sides. A Knight draws his sword. When the others see this, they are charged with swords drawn. The battle was intense, Knights falling on both sides. I am stuck in my right shoulder with the Knight's heavy sword, my arm almost severed. I fight on with one arm and slay the Knight who struck my arm. Sir Archer's Knights were prevailing. Their enemy was retreating but not Sir Archer whose arrow struck me in the left eye and knocked me off my horse. Another Knight strikes me in my leg, and he brings me to my knees. At the same time, the Knight spins and strikes me again and decapitates me. The true version of the battle was the Knight was bitten by an adder and drew his sword to kill the snake, A MISTAKE. Before my death, I heard the woman curse again and I saw a bright light.

CHAPTER TWO

CAPTAIN MICHAEL "MIKE" O'TOOLE FROM BUTTE MONTANA, SON OF JAMES AND ANN O'TOOLE

Butte Montana: There is Gold in them there hills, the Butte Boom.

Until late 1880, copper was used only for pots and plain roofing material and ornamental decorations. When the electrical industry spread, so did the demand for copper. Every industrial city in the world was installing streetlights. People wanted electricity in their homes. In 1882, Marcus Daly came across a deposit of copper in a silver camp of Butte Montana. The deposit found by Daly found in a large hill called Butte Hill contained 35 percent of copper. Butte would supply 41 percent of the world's copper. Daly had plans for Butte. He constructed a smelting plant. He recruited workers from all over the world—Finland, Ireland, China—to work in these emerging cities. The ethnic groups formed small communities like Dublin Gulch in Butte, the new home for Jack and Ann O' Toole, my parents.

My parents came to Butte from West Cork Ireland. My father had experience in the copper mine and many of his friends had already gone to Butte. He would join them. There are three hundred mines operating within the boundary of Butte that became known fondly as Hell Raising Gulch. Butte never slept, had a reputation of being America's toughest town.

Michael "Mike" O'Toole born March 5, 1898 to Jack and Ann O'Toole in Butte Montana lived in a community, Dublin Gulch. I was born at midnight and had some complications with being born small. I was early; my mother blamed Butte and never got over it. I had what they called a birthmark on my face. It caused a deformity on my forehead that got worse as I aged. It defined my social life because I had no friends. I spent most of my youth with my mother, reading, and learning. When I was in eighth grade, I made friends and we spent a lot of time together in the dumps. That is what most kids did. I hated it. You got dirty and this would upset my mother. I hated Butte, it is dirty everywhere you look, smoke, loud noise, and trains coming and going. It's dark in the daylight. The night shift whistle would blow so you knew what time it was without looking at a clock. At a shift change, I remember the miners walking home. They had a medicinal smell when they came up from the dryer (miner changing room). They would shower there; they must have used the same soap. I was a newsboy at shift change. It was time to hustle to the street corners to sell my papers. My clothes were always dirty, which was despair to my mother who washes them. I remember light yellow dirt, when it got wet from rain or snow it would stick to your shoes or clothes like glue. When I came home with it all over me, I was in trouble and a date with a razor strap. I remember wanting out of Butte. Most of the kids were going to follow their fathers into the mines, not me, I hated it. I found freedom in books. My way out of Butte was education according to my teachers. That would by my focus, school. I was on my way to high school and I was ready. I was a great student at Butte High on high honor roll, the debate team, played some sports. My social life did not change, no girlfriend, no real friends. Most had given up on their studies, accepting the fate of a future in the mines, the dirt, the smell, the miner's future. I was in town and met a marine officer who was talking to some people at the restaurant. I found out it was his family, and he was home on leave. I asked him if I could talk to him after his dinner and he invited me to sit down. I did, and as he told stories of travel and life he served. I asked how I could join. He said he would take me when I was ready. Graduation was next week. My plans were made. My parents were expecting college to be my future. They were so proud of how well I did. It was time to tell them I wanted to be a Marine Officer. That would be my future. They were upset, yelling for the first time in my life, my mom crying begging me to not go. I think that was the first time I disappointed my parents. I joined the USMC the next day.

I had orders to Marine base at Quantico trench warfare, something we all heard about. The training was intense. We learned what trench warfare was and we thought we knew what to expect. Every Marine heading to the western front lines went through Quantico to prepare for their survival in Europe in 1917. Trench war was nothing I could have imagined, miles of trenches; masses of Marines huddled together in constant water and mud dying from small arms fire artillery, snipers picking us off one at a time, enemy infiltrating barbed wire and the smell of dead bodies between our line and the Germans. We called it No Man's Land because no man could survive there. The General's repeating tactical failures resulted in loss of Marines. The Germans and we witness the results of an industrial backed war. When I arrived at the Western Front, I reported to duty and was assigned a company of one hundred marines. The trench was six foot to ten foot wide and just as high. Parapets along the trench spared at regular intervals. These served as machine gun or sniper nest and guard post. Grenade sumps were dug in the trench bottom for extra protection from enemy grenades. A trench was dug in a zigzagging pattern along much of the front lines to protect men from an infiltration of the enemy into the trench and provided some cover for both hand-to-hand fighting and small arms fire. Barbed wire was used along the front lines to impede the enemy when they attacked. We needed to replace the wire both as we advanced and when the enemy would breach our wire. I lost a lot of my men in this task. The German sharpshooters we would pick them off. Some would be caught up in the wire and then are shot. We could only advance one hundred yards at a time. Some days we would advance and some we would retreat. I lost fifty Marines in the months we were in the trench. No one came out the way they went in. Most suffered trench foot from standing in water and being wet all the time. The rotation from the front to the rear, you never knew if this was your last rotation to the front line.

When I got orders to report to the 4th Marine 2nd division, I welcomed it. I lost fifty Marines in the trench. I was going on the offensive.

June 1, 1918, two division troops were dug in along a defense line just north of a village when I was told to withdraw and retreat. My response was retreat hell we just got here. The morale in my men was unsure because of the uncertainty: the 5th Marines in the west, and the 6th Marines in the east. The 2nd division and the 5th Marines show the Germans what long distance warfare was all about.

June 4, 1918, determined German assault against the Americans line was turned back. There had been a failure on the right flank by second division and by the 5th Marines around Les Mares and the first division failure near Clampillon. The reason the German attack failed was heavy guns and artillery and machine guns had arrived. My men were hungry; their kitchens were still stuck on the road in the mud. The failure of the attack on June 4 was known as the high-water mark German offensive; it was the closest the Germans got to Paris, fifty miles away.

June 6, 1918: This was the most catastrophic day in the Marine Corps history to date. There were two attacks at 0500. Both attacks were successfully repelled. Despite no preparation and poor timing, we pulled it off with only two companies. A timely arrival of two more companies avoided sure defeat. Twelve hours later, battalions of the 5th and 6th Marine Regiments attack the front and the woods from the south and west. They captured the village of Borsches. The lack of coordinated attack on the woods left us struggling to get into the southern edge of the woods. We entered the village with only lead elements of our company, keeping the village proved to be difficult. Our flanks were wide open fields. Any attempt to reinforce them received heavy German fire. My men bravely kept Marines supplied with cover fire. We were just outnumbered. LT JG SMITH OF THE USN RECEIVES THE MEDAL OF HONOR AFTER BEING KILLED TRYING TO SAVE CAPTAIN MICHAEL "MIKE" O'TOOLE engaged a German machine gun and was killed June 6, 1918. As I am dying, I am aware of a Knight and a curse and a bright light with something. The curse of the Red Rose.

CHAPTER THREE

THE SIX DAY WAR

HAIFA

At the beginning of the twentieth century, Haifa emerged as an industrial port city and growing population center. The Haifa railway was established at that time. The Haifa district was home to approximately twenty thousand inhabitants, ninety percent Arab with eighty two percent Muslim, fourteen percent Christian and four percent Jewish. As Aliyah (immigration of Jews) increased, the balance shifted by 1945. The population was fifty-three percent Arab with thirty-three percent Muslim, twenty percent

Christian and forty seven percent Jewish.
Haifa was designated as part of the Jewish
State in 1947. As part of the United Nations
partition plan that proposed dividing Man-
dated Palestine into two states in December
1947, the Jewish militant group, Iran,
hurled two bombs at a group of Arabs
working on the construction of refineries in
Haifa killing six Arabs and injuring forty-
two. Rioting erupted in which two thousand Arab employees were killed and
thirty-nine of their Jewish colleagues in
what has become known as the Haifa Oil
Refinery Massacre.

In May 1941, Iraqi fascists backed by pop-
ular support tried to overthrow the
pro-western majority and seize the British
oil field in Iraq to facilitate the oil-dependent
German advance east to Russia. That failed.
The Iraqi coup plotters in Baghdad decided
to do the next best thing, exterminate its
Jews in a single blow. Jews were ordered to
stay in their homes, and their doors were
marked with red hams. At the last minute,
the extermination plot fell apart. But as the
coup leaders fled, in that momentary power
vacuum from June 1 to 2, 1941, dejected
swarms of soldiers in concert with police,

common criminals, and nondescript mobs rampaged through Baghdad hunting for Jews. They were easily found. Swords and rifles, some decapitated, cut down hundreds of Jews. Babies were sliced in half and thrown into the Tights River. Girls were raped in front of their parents. Parents were mercilessly killed in front of their children. The merciless aspersion continued the day after Israel declared its independence on May 15, 1948. The new nation was divided from all sides by Armies constructed by most of the Arab states. It was not termed a war of liberation by the Arab leadership, but a war of extermination. The Iraqi military saw limited action. The Arab armies were rich in numbers, and rich in death rhetoric. They were poorly organized and were not ready to fight. Israel could not be defeated; all the nations involved signed a United Nations negotiated implemented armistice with Egypt. Only Iraq refused to sign, demanding to stay at war. As a result of that war, Israel now controlled even more of the Palestine land after July 19, 1948. Iraq amended Penal Code 51, which stated anarchy, immorality and communism adding the word Zionist. Every Jew was thereby criminalized. It only took two Muslim witnesses to denounce a Jew. With virtually no avenue to appeal, Joseph and Elizabeth Kamal with nothing but the clothes on their backs became refugees from Iraq to Israel. Joseph was experienced in oil so they settled in Haifa and he found work. Their lives were much harder in their new country. He would always talk about how proud he was to be part of this new country, a Jewish State. He would speak out about how much he hated Iraq. Elizabeth would long for her life in her much-loved Iraq, her friends and relatives that she lost touch with. She was upset all the time because she left her friends and relatives behind when they decided to leave. With no contact at all, she feared they were imprisoned or dead; this all contributed to her poor health.

March 7, 1948 Alts Kamal was born to Joseph and Elizabeth Kamal. A little girl was born with an ugly scar on her forehead from the instruments the doctors had to use for a breech birth. Or at least that was my parents' story. As I got older, I doubted that is what it was. I always believed that my father was disappointed with a daughter. He had wanted a son. He believed that his beloved new country would be better served by a son because the New Jewish State was going to face many problems. The dreams of so many Jews that their nation was going to be neutral in world affairs, like the Switzerland of the Middle East, and welcome all to live in peace and avoid wars was not realistic. My father believed that Israel's defense would be her most important priority and that would require the loss of blood and lives. He felt that a son would better serve the needs of his country. Since my mother's complication with my birth, she could not have more children. My father, too old to serve, was guarded with me and my path was selected for me so not to hurt his beloved wife and mother of his only child. From a young age, I wished I was the son he wanted and was determined to prove that my gender would not define my contribution to my beloved country. I would prove myself not only to the country that I loved but to my father. As a child growing up, there was a constant awareness of the conflict between my Jewish friends and the Palestinian kids. We were enemies living on the same mountain or street. We live together but were enemies and both prepared for a conflict that was waiting around the next house or road.

I grew hardened by the conflict. I would talk with my father; he would tell me the story repeatedly about what brought him and my mom to Israel and how we were tasked by our Jewish history. The plight of the Jewish people is to die, if necessary, to protect our home, our land, our Nation, our future. An obligation we all have as a Jew. I strived for more information, more history of the Jewish people. I wanted to stone every non-Jew I encountered. I heard of a high school that Jews from all over Israel could attend. I was an Israeli and my country would open new frontiers that were closed since 1948.

I was an average student in most of my studies. I did very well in history and was at the top of my class in computer science and engineering. I won awards in both engineering and computer science along with an opportunity to attend Telavi University secondary school, a high school located in Herzliya. The school was established in 1960, thanks to a donation. As a high school belonging to the Telavi University, the school offered only science electives—Computer Science, Engineering, and Biotechnology. One of the main reasons I wanted to attend Telavi University secondary school is because it was known to be the school from which the greatest number of career soldier students graduated from compared to all other Israel's schools. I wanted a career in the military as a soldier. I accept my obligation to defend Israel, preserve the Jewish Nation, honor my Jewish history, and make my father proud of his daughter and to show future daughters of Israel a path of contribution. I would be the best; my gender would have nothing to do with it. School was very hard; I was competing against the best students in Israel. I made many mistakes and was close to failing. My engineering classes were my best. I excelled to the top of my class. By the time I was in my last year, and with my obligation of service in the military, I wanted to go to the paratrooper brigade which is part of the Israel Defense Force and perform a lot of Special Force style missions.

33rd brigade is known as PUB (paratroopers brigade within the Israel Defense Forces "IDF" and forms a major part of the infantry corps). It has a history of carrying out Special Forces missions. The Paratroop brigade soldiers wore maroon braids with an infantry pin and reddish-brown boots. I was both excited and scared when I got off the bus onto the training field. My thoughts went to my father; would he be proud or disappointed? Could he accept that his only child was reporting to the tip of the sword? That she will fight for the Jewish Nation to honor the history of Jewish people. The first week was the introduction. A lot of paperwork, meetings, testing physical fitness, running, and marching, they called the "weed out process". Our company reported there were one hundred recruits down from the five hundred, all cut for various reasons. Not that it mattered there were five females. Our instructors were seasoned military and looked the part. They expected us to conduct ourselves as a military. This wasn't new for us. They had no patience for any exception, they hit us hard. They had us in ten straight lines, ten recruits in each. When they said "sound off" one through ten, I looked, and they moved all the females in the first row. I thought we were there because we were females and there to compete among each other. The General was in front, he said you are lined up by your scores. Starting to my left call out starting with the number one, I heard one; two, three, four and I called out five and the numbers continued. All I could think was, if my father could see me now. I knew now I had ninety-five brothers focusing on my back that will push me harder than I ever thought possible. The instructors seem to have one goal, break us, and make us quit. In the first month twenty-five quit, three were women. Now I am number two with only seventy-five still here with four weeks left. The next four weeks will be about paratroopers learning how to navigate through jump school. You learn to operate while falling out of the sky into all types of scenarios; none easy. We lost thirty-five more paratroopers. Some sent back because of broken legs and ankles some just would not jump, they just froze. Two women are still here with only one week to go, the worst week. Only forty paratroopers left. The last week is survival week. We were dropped out in the desert with limited supplies. Two groups of paratroopers are twenty kilometers apart. I am leading unit two and number one is leading unit one. Our orders are to link up and assault an ammo depot. All we have is our compass and the coordinates of our target. First, we must find and link up both units. We have no coordinates for the other unit. The desert took its toll; we lost five to the elements. They had to be choppered out. We knew the target was to our south. We were twelve kilometers to our target. We were told the distance between the units was twenty kilometers. We had a disagreement on where unit one might be. My second in command thought they would be coming from the east. My gut told me they were ten miles further to the south. If I am right, we link up at the target. If I am wrong, we would arrive ahead of unit one and have to defeat the ammo depot with only one unit. The decision could be the end for me. I ordered unit two to move to the south. We had a homing device that would turn on when we were one kilometer apart. When we were within one kilometer the homing device signed on. I was right. We defeated the ammo depot. Unit one lost ten men to the elements. Both females made it; we would become great friends and then we became more than friends. We fell in love and both of us would be paratroopers. How will this work? We graduated number one and two. I was number one and she was number two. Turns out only losing five men in unit one and her losing ten men in unit two resulted in more points for me. I passed her and became group commander. This made for great pillow talk or maybe pillow fights. We both were waiting for orders and hoped we would be close. Against regulation, we were not in the same command. We would keep in touch. I had orders to the 33rd brigade and her orders didn't come through yet. I was on my way to lead a company of paratroopers. Now would my father be proud of his little girl. Who needs a son? He has me.

THE SIX DAY WAR

The Six Day War was a brief but bloody conflict during June 1967 between Israel and the Arab states of Egypt, Syria, and Jordan. Following years of diplomatic friction and skirmishes between Israel and its neighbors, Israel Defense Forces launched preemptive air strikes that crippled the air forces of Egypt and its allies. Israel then staged a successful ground offensive and seized the Sinai Peninsula and the Gaza Strip. The west bank and east Jerusalem were taken from Jordon and the Golden Height from Syria. The brief war ended with a U.N. brokered ceasefire, but significantly altered the map of the Middle East and gave rise to lingering geopolitical friction. The Six Day War came on the heels of several decades of political tension and military conflict between Israel and the Arab states. In 1948, following a dispute surrounding the founding of Israel, a coalition of Arab nations had launched a failed invasion of the nascent Jewish state as part of the first Arab Israel War. A second major conflict known as the Suez Crisis erupted in 1956, when Israel, the United Kingdom and France staged a controversial attack on Egypt in response to Egyptian President's, General Abdel Nasser, nationalization of the Suez Canal. An era of relative calm prevailed in the Middle East during the late 1950s and early 1960 but the political situation continued to rest on edge. Arab leaders were aggrieved by their military losses. As a result of the 1948 War, hundreds of thousands of Palestinian refugees were created by Israel's victory. Meanwhile, many Israelis were confined to believe they faced an existential threat from Egypt and other Arab nations. By the end of the 1960's, a series of border disputes were the major spark for the Six Day War. Syrian backed Palestinian guerillas had begun staging attacks across the Israel borders, provoking reprisal raids from the Israeli defense forces. In April 1967, the skirmishes worsened after Israel and Syria fought a ferocious air and artillery engagement in which six Syrian fighter jets were destroyed. In the wake of the April air battle, the Soviet Union provided Egypt with intelligence that Israel was moving troops to its northern border with Syria, in preparation for a full-scale invasion. The information was inaccurate but it nevertheless stirred Egyptian President General Abdel Nasser into action. In a show of support for his Syrian allies, he ordered Egyptian forces to advance into the Sinai Peninsula. They expelled a United Nation peacekeeping force that had been guarding the border with Israel for over a decade. In the days that followed, Nasser continued to rattle the saber. On May 22, he banned Israel's shipping from the Straits of Tiran, the sea passage connecting the Red Sea and the Gulf of Aqaba. A week later, the international military operation to reopen the Strait of Tiran. The plan never materialized. By early June 1967 Israel's leaders had voted to counter the Arab military buildup by launching preemptive strikes. The Israel Defense forces initiated operation forces, a coordinated aerial attack on Egypt. That morning some two hundred warplanes took off from Israel and swooped west over the Mediterranean before converging on Egypt from the north. After catching the Egyptian's by surprise, they assaulted eighteen different airfields and eliminated roughly ninety percent of the Egyptian Air Force as it sat on the ground. Israel then expanded the range of its attack and decimated the Air Force of Jordan, Syria and Iraq by the end of the day on June 5, 1967. Israeli pilots had won full control of the skies over the Middle East. Israel all but secured victory by establishing air superiority, but fierce fighting continued for several more days. The ground war in Egypt began June 5. In concert with the air strikes, Israeli tanks and infantry stormed across the border and into the Sinai Peninsula and the Gaza Strip. Egyptian forces put up a spirited resistance, but later fell into disarray after Field Marshal Abdel Hakim Amir ordered a general retreat over the next several days. Israeli forces pursued the routed Egyptians across the Sinai inflicting severe casualties on June 10, 1967. A United Nations brokered ceasefire took effect and the Six Day War came to an abrupt end. It was later estimated that some twenty thousand

Arabs and eight hundred Israeli's had died in just 132 hours of fighting.

BATTLE OF ABU-ANGELIA 1967

The Israeli attack plan was based on intelligence gathered two days before it was started, which indicated Um-Kata was defended by only one infantry battalion. Based on the information, the Israelis planned a frontal attack by their reinforced independent tank battalions. After aerial bombardment, this tank battalion started its attack on Um-Kata on June 5 at 08:15. The attack ceased to a halt however, due to resistance from an unknown Egyptian formation and an unknown minefield causing the loss of seven Israeli centurions. New orders for the independent tank battalion were to break off the attack and then attack from the north through the sand dunes. After a short aerial bombardment, the 14th armored brigade and two tank battalions, super Sherman and two armored infantry battalions in halftracks were ordered to attack further south. This attack began at 12:30 but was forced to a halt as well. Now that the strength and positions of the Egyptians were known, General Arial Sharon changed his plans. The independent tank battalion was ordered to drive through the sand dunes following a camel path and attack the Egyptians. Armed at the Urata Dam at the same time, the 14th armored brigade would attack from the east. Before this could happen, Um-Kata would have to be taken; a task given to General Sharon's infantry brigade which was held in reserve up until then. This infantry attack was to occur under the cover of darkness following a secondary approach to Um-Kata through the dunes. Meanwhile the Israeli armored divisions would provide support to all Israeli artillery, making the Israeli infantry extremely vulnerable. It was decided that the Egyptian artillery would be taken out of action prior to the attack using the brigade of paratroopers. With only six helicopters available, only a limited number of units could be used. Meanwhile, the independent tank battalion was engaged by the Egyptian defenders in the sand dunes by 16:00 and was able to continue to their positions near Abu-Avella and the Urata Dam. At 18:00 the Infantry Brigade was in place. At around 23:00, while the paratroopers were discovered and fired upon by Egyptian artillery, they made it to their attack positions. Major Alta Kamal was in charge of the units flying in the six helicopters. My orders were to drop behind the artillery line and destroy them. The enemy wasn't currently engaged with our infantry. I knew if they discovered us, in our descent, it would be deadly. I was in the first helicopter with nine men. The other five helicopters had ten in each. Sixty paratroopers against a large enemy artillery force. As we dropped in, the first unit was fired upon, it seemed like as soon as we cleared the helicopter. I was in front, circling down, weapons at the ready. The first unit made it in. No wind to speak of, so we landed on target. We took cover behind the dunes to provide cover for the other units. All units made it on target, no injuries I was feeling confident. We rallied and moved in what I believed was behind the artillery line. I was mistaken; we were off center a little to their left flank and this would create difficulty engaging without taking on heavy enemy fire. I decided to lead the first unit into a better firing position. We collected all our mortar rounds, from all six units and moved out. We covered about half the distance and they opened up. Since we were off course on our descent, we didn't see what was protecting their flank, two mortar bunkers and a company of men. We lost three men at the first exchange. We needed to get mortars firing sending rounds on their position. I picked up the mortar bags and started sending mortar on their location. We had the advantage. We were in position on top of a large sand dune above them so we were having success. We eliminated the mortar bunker and held their troops down allowing our artillery to engage. We were taking a huge toll. The enemy started to advance; they were charging the dune. I called the location and that they were advancing. It was too late they were too close for our artillery support. If they fired, we would all be killed. We decided to fight until the rest of the units arrived. There were seven against fifty. We were all part of the Special Forces, had better equipment and were better trained. We cut the oncoming force in half. They were within meters. We went to small arms fire and made every shot count. Still reducing the oncoming ranks, my men fought and we could hear the units coming from behind us. We knew it would be minutes until the other units would be here, we just might make it.

There is a white light, a soldier with a scar, saying THE CURSE OF THE RED ROSE and something so shining, Major Alta Kamal killed from enemy mortar fire along with six of her men.

CHAPTER FOUR

THE CREEK INDIAN WAR

LIFE AS A CREEK INDIAN

I was born to Scenanki (Meaning Flower) Chitte (Meaning Brave) November 4, 1795. I was the third child. I had two brothers, Hasseola (Meaning Rising Son) he was seven winters old and Latmochattee (Meaning Red Eagle) he was five winters old. I was born healthy and strong; the only exception was an ugly distorted face due to a large gash in my forehead. My mother was so protective; she named me Schoy (Meaning Beauty). When I was older, this name would cause a lot of teasing. My grandmother would encourage me to see myself as my mother sees me. I would learn to do that and it built a lot of strength. My brothers were older and living with my uncle was like the Creek custom. My uncle, Helatche, (Meaning War Chief) was teaching them to hunt, fish, and the use of weapons in battle, the bow and knife and their red club. They both were preparing for their session to become adults. They are still too young and doing very well. I would see them in practice and wished I could train with them; but not possible. I must follow the ways of a woman and my grandmother and mother would be my trainers. I would see my brothers at the training field. They would tease me. I would be sad, even sick. All I wanted is to be an adult so I could stop the teasing. Even now I could hear my mother's voice saying how beautiful I was, I could feel my confidence slipping away. I had to wait for my session to become an adult. I would ask my mother when I could go. Her answer was always the same when you stop acting like a child. That meant stop complaining, get after my teaching with my grandmother, and learn the duties of a Creek woman. My grandmother's stories were so interesting. All I wanted to do is listen to her. I started training picking corn, making baskets, learning to prepare meals, and making clothing and cleaning the cabin. I followed my mother and grandmother everywhere they went. I was determined to be an adult. My grandmother's name was Eyota (Meaning Great). My grandmother's teaching would also include her stories about her life and the battles she witnessed and the loss of family and tribe members. She also told stories about good times; our land, what the Creek people accomplished against other tribes, and governments' armies. I should feel proud to be a Creek. Her teachings made me want to make my grandmother proud of me. I would work hard to honor her. Sometimes my grandfather, Chikggilli (Meaning Chief), would let me listen to his teachings. He spoke of the loss of his warriors. He had many braves in his charge. He would tell stories about battles against the Americans, who broke their treaties and continue to break the Indian line and take our land. That generation of Creeks farmed. He stressed that we must protect what our ancestors' spirits who were among us and in secret burial land who fought and died for our land. We would not let the Americans take what was rightly ours. He spoke about the British and the French who were fighting against the Americans and the White Sticks, the northern Creeks, to stop the Americans from taking our land. He had warned us of future battles that would be bloody and might wipe out the Creek Nation as we knew it. He asks if there were women who wanted to train with him as possible warriors to help stop the Americans. We did not always train. Sometimes we played a game, called Afvcketv pronounced (ah-fuich-kitt-uh), a stickball game. All adults played the game they loved and some even made bets on the game. This was my fourteenth winter, so it is time for my session. A session is the Creek's passage from childhood to being an adult. I was going into the woods to live for seven moons and would prove if I survive, I would be an adult. My mother and grandmother had trained me for this test and thought I was ready so tomorrow I would leave. The first day after the long hike I must make shelter, find water and find food. Half of the light of the day was gone. I had to work fast. The cold was coming in and I needed a fire to stay alive. I was able to build a small fire, then a shelter, a bed, and killed a small rabbit for dinner. The first moon came; six more moons would I make it? When it got so bad, I would hear my grandmother telling her stories and my mother telling me how much she loved me. The last day would be the worst. When I lay in my swamp weeds I used for a bed, it was a dark moon so I couldn't see. I heard a terrible noise, loud and close. I awoke and grabbed my weapons and was face to face with a large bear. Expecting the bear to charge but he didn't. He stood and just looked at me. We were eye to eye. He could have killed me with one blow. He just stood there watching me and then turned and ran away. When my session was over, during my walk back to my village, I was remembering the bear that visited me in the wilderness. When I went to my grandmother, I told her of my visit by the bear. She said that no Creek can pass to adulthood without a vision or experience like yours. You are no longer a child; you are adult Creek.

The paths in front of me were clear; find a Creek warrior and start a family. The problem was who would want me with my ugly face. My father was a powerful man, Our Chief, and my mother and grandmother said many families in our village would be proud to be part of our family. How many times have your mother and I told you to see yourself as we see you, as a beautiful Creek woman who will make the entire Creek people proud? I was introduced to a young Creek warrior, his name Talofhanjo, (Meaning Crazy Bear). I will always know that my grandfather arranged this. I was sure when he looked at me, he would run. He didn't. He looked at me with eyes I've seen before; those deep eyes of calm the eyes of the bear that visited me the last day of my session. Our lives in the village were happy. We lived in a cabin next to my family. Our warriors were gone a lot in battles fighting with the French. We liked the French warriors who took Creek wives. We wore their clothes, and some moved into the village. Our village was growing a lot with many children. When our warriors were away, the younger women had to protect the village from white militiamen who would come and try to take our children and young women. They would rape and kill the women and give the children to family who lived on plantations. I learned to fight and kill the whites who came for us. We lost some of our children and young women to these attacks.

On December 23, 1812, my son was born and we named him Huhuewahehle, (Meaning Good Child). We were happy and the family was helping raise him. There were times all the family would be in the cabin together. We would hear the construction of the new fort being constructed close to our village. In the winter, our warriors stayed in the village more. We were afraid of an attack.

THE CREEK INDIAN WAR 1813-1814

The Creek Indian War was a regional war between opposing Creek fractions, European empires, and the United States taking place along the Gulf Coast. Major conflicts of the war took place between state military units and the "Red Sticks" Creek. The Creek War was considered part of the War of 1812. Mostly, it was concurrent with the American British War and had many of the participants. The Red Sticks had sought the British support and aided Admiral Cochrane's advance toward New Orleans. The Choctaw War began as a conflict with the Creek Confederation, but local white militia units quickly became involved. British traders in Florida as well as the Spanish government provided the Red Sticks with arms and supplies because of their shared interest in preventing the expansion of the United States into their areas. The United States Government formed an alliance with the Choctaw nation and Cherokee Nation (the traditional enemies of the Creek) along with the remaining Creeks to put down the rebellion. The war effectively ended with the treaty of Fort Jackson (August 1814) when General Andrew Jackson forced the Creek Confederacy to surrender more than twenty-one million acres in what is now southern Georgia and central Alabama. During and after the American Revolution, the United States wished to maintain the Indian line, which had been established by the Proclamation of 1763. The Indian line created a boundary for colonial settlement in order to prevent illegal encroachment into Indian lands and also helped the United States Government maintain control over the Indian trade. Traders and settlers often violate the terms of the treaties establishing the Indian line The United States used this encroachment as one argument to expand its territory. Those increasing territory gains, westward into Creek territory, compelled the British and Spanish governments to strengthen existing alliances with the Creek.

BATTLE OF TALLASEEHATCHEE

The Battle of Tallaseehatchee was fought during the War of 1812 and the Creek War of November 3, 1813, in Alabama between Native American Red Stick Creeks and the United States Troops. A Calvary Force was commanded by Brigadier General John Coffee and was able to defeat the Creek warriors.

After the massacre at Fort Mims, General Andrew Jackson assembled an Army of two thousand and five hundred Tennessee Militia. Jackson began marching into Mississippi territory to combat the Red Stick Creeks. Jackson's troops began to construct Fort Struthers along the Coosa River fifteen miles (twenty-four kilometers) away from the Fort Mims lay the Creek village of Tallaseehatchee where a sizable force of Red Stick warriors was. Jackson ordered his friend and most trusted subordinate, General John Coffee, to attack the village. He divided his brigade into two columns that encircled the village, two companies ventured into the center of the village to draw out the Creek warriors. The trap worked. The Creek warriors attacked and were forced to retreat back into the buildings of the village. General Coffee closed the circle on the trapped Creek warriors. The Creek scouts ran back to the village to prepare for an attack from a column of soldiers. Our warriors went out fighting in the training field. They had to retreat back into the cabins. When they did, more soldiers were all around, firing into the cabins. My family was dying all around me. My mother died first, shot in the head, my father and brothers went back outside trying to protect the cabin. They were massacred. My husband lays his baby son and me down. He lies in front of us to protect us from getting shot. He was hit many times. He dies holding my hand. I am hit in the legs and move my baby behind me, then the shooting stops. The door opens; a man with a rifle enters. He walks up to me and picks up my son, who is crying and screaming. He holds my baby, points his musket at me and fires. I see three shadow images all saying the curse of the rose. I see a shining piece of metal. Sehoy died November 3, 1813.

Coffee's forces killed 186 warriors, as well as many women and children, while suffering only five dead and forty-one wounded, one child given to Andrew Jackson.

David Crocket, serving in a Tennessee militia, who served with Coffee, commented "We shot them down like dogs". In his memoirs, he also describes participating in burning down a house where forty-six Creek warriors had taken refuge.

CHAPTER FIVE

THE BATTLE OF WAKE ISLAND

Daisuke was born to Akio (father) and Hinata (Mother) in Kure Kaikokan (Port of Kure) Japan, 1925. The location of Kure is within the inland Sea of Japan. This was considered important in controlling the sea-lanes around western Japan. Kure was established as the second Naval District and its harbor was dredged. A breakwater construction and docking facilities for warships were constructed.

My father was a construction worker who worked on dredging the harbor and the construction of docking. Kure dockyard recorded a number of significant engineering accomplishments; in 1905 the launching

of the first major domestically built battleship, the cruiser Tsukuba and in 1940 the
launching of the largest battleship ever built,
the Yamato. The Imperial Japanese's Naval
Academy and Naval Staff College were re-
located in 1890 From Tokyo to nearby
Etajima in 1920. The Japanese Navy established its main submarine base and
submarine warfare training school in Kure
and its air wing was established in 1932 and
a telecommunications center in 1937.

My childhood as I am the only son was that
I lived with my parents and was expected to
live in their home and provide for them.
Living in a busy port city was interesting. A
lot of my friends got work loading and un-
loading ships. I could not because of my
mother's health and my disability. I have a scar
over both of my eyes. My mother was protective and kept me home to do my chores
and study. She believed I should be educated
and forced my father to get books from
around the world. I would learn English,
French, and Mandarin. It was very hard to
learn. Math was easy. I had my own abacus
from Spain. My father would take me to the
shipyard and explain the different ships; what
they did and how they did it, even the

warships. When I was thirteen years old, my parents were killed in a house fire. I survived. My obligation to care from them was no longer needed. I had no one, no family, no home; I was alone. The company my father worked at knew of my studies and spoke to the Naval Academy on my behalf to enroll me in The Staff College. The college was a maritime school. Most of my studies prepared me for naval service. I never thought I could get in the Navy because of my forehead but I applied anyway. While at the college, the quality of food was better and I started to grow. I was already taller than all of my classmates but I kept growing, getting bigger and stronger. At the end of my last year, I had grown to 1.88 meters tall and weighed 93.44 kilograms. My classmates called me Giant. The Navy wanted me to be Japanese Marine. I accepted my assignment and would report in one week.

I reported to Special Naval Landing Forces (SNLF). My training would be in Kure, Maizuru, Sasebo, and Yokosuka. The SNLF had a lot of success fighting in China and all-over Southeast Asia. The unit's success comes from their training in compact Naval Training for operations at Sea, hand-to-hand fighting to the death. The number one responsibility was the defense of troops in forward positions, defending bunkers. When training started, I noticed one common trait. All of the men standing at muster were all over 1.88 meters tall, not common for Japanese men. The first base was Yokosuka Japan. Combat training, physical training, and weapons training early in the course of the next couple weeks would start with class work and physical training, which I found difficult and challenging. During weapons training, I excelled and the top shot in camp with a number of different weapons. The area I got noticed in was with sniper weapons. I passed the test and the training and have orders to go to Sasebo paratroop school; something I had no experience in and was very nervous about. This could be what stops me and sends me to the fleet or the Army. The first couple of weeks were all about ground training and packing my parachute landing without getting hurt or worse. The men who pass this move to the jump platform. Each of us is on a platform thirteen meters high to practice our landing without getting hurt. I was surprised how hard you hit the ground. A lot of men broke their legs or feet. We are starting to jump for real out of planes for the first time. They say if you don't jump the men behind you will just push you out. All the men were scared, some talking about quitting. This was not an option, jump or fall, your choice. The jump went well. I was in the last seat on the left side of the plane. We take off. We arrive at jump altitude; we are ordered to stand and hook up to the jump line. The man in front of me gets to the door and stops. I push him and then exit. I would experience this fear many times; always having the same nerves, then calm, then the fear of the landing. I passed parachute school. Orders to Maizuru, hand-to-hand combat fighting with swords and knives. Most Japanese men are taught martial arts, me included, so the hand-to-hand was to see what we knew. Most of us were trained to use it as defense, not to attack, so it had to be taught to kill fast and efficiently. It was intense. We became experts in killing quickly with our hands, knives and swords; the unit did well. Everyone passed, moving to the final school for me back home, Kure Maritime School.

The Naval school was a lot of classroom learning; star charting, navigation knots, firefighting on ship and defense against fighting at sea to protect against ship loss to the enemy. Shore landing was where we spent the majority of our efforts. We would make countless practice landings under bad weather, high seas, and fire with live shells blasting all around us. We learn that team-work was the only way possible to accomplish the landing. We all had one test left, the swim with our gear from four kilometers out to sea and return to the beach. Once there, they capture a bunker with a live machine gun. To graduate we must accomplish this mission. Our unit passed; others didn't, and they would need to start over.

After graduation, I received orders to the South Seas Force, which included the light cruiser, Yubari, six Destroyers, two Momi-Class Destroyers, converted to patrol boats and my ship, Kinryu Maru and our sister ship Kongo Maru containing 450 Special Naval Landing Force Troops.

The battle of Wake Island happened simultaneously with the attack on Pearl Harbor, the morning of December 7, 1941(7 December in Hawaii). Hawaii is on the opposite side of the International Date Line.

FIRST LANDING ATTEMPT

At sunrise on the morning of December 11, the Garrison, with the support of the four remaining Wildcats, repelled our landing of the South Seas Force including our ships and two submarines patrolling nearby securing our perimeter. The U.S. Marines fired at the invasion fleet with their six, five-inch (127-millimeter) cost-defense guns. Major Kelly, the Garrison Commander Fisher, ordered the gunners to hold their fire until we moved within range of the coastal defense. We lost two destroyers with all hands but one survivor, me. I got picked up by a Boat 33 patrol boat that was being used as a landing craft for 225 Special Naval Landing force. We recorded our first defeat against the Americans, the first setback of the war against them.

After the Initial raid was fought off, American news media reported that there were queries about supplies and reinforcements. Commander Fisher was reported to have said "send us more Japs". In fact, Fisher requested resupply and equipment including gunsights, spare parts and fire control radar to his Commander of the 14 Naval District.

Our sea siege and our frequent air attacks on the Wake Garrison continued without re-supply for the Americans.

THE SECOND ASSAULT

The initial resistance staged by the Garrison required our Navy to detach the second carrier division, three Cruisers and two destroyers all fresh from Pearl Harbor. Our second assault came December 23. It consisted of the ships from the first assault plus 1500 Marines. The landing began at 02:30. After early bombardment, the Patrol number thirty-two and my boat patrol boat number thirty-three, we beached and burned both boats. We made it ashore. We had a unit of some 400 men. We advanced and hit very light resistance. When we cleared the beach, the Americans were dug in. They were outnumbered but were holding their position, largely holding down our advance. Because two machine gun bunkers are placed up the hill under a ridge of rocks hidden. Our orders are to take out the bunkers. We split off the unit, my unit in charge of the right bunker, 900 meters up the hill. We throw artillery at them, not effective. We have to destroy with small arms and we have to get close. Seems to be the only option. We move forward with cover. I advance to within meters to the position lying on my back with the machine gun fire going out over my right side I hear a large explosion to my left. If I try to raise my weapon, I am dead. I decided to try to throw a grenade into the bunker. First, I see a white light with four figures all chanting THE CURSE OF THE RED ROSE, they are holding something metal with red and gold.

Daisuke was killed in action December 25, 1941.

CHAPTER SIX

BATTLES OF SHAMAR, PART OF THE AFGHANISTAN WAR 1979–1989

Shisha and Shani Kahn moved to the city of Kabul on August 18, 1954. Shani is with child and her daughter, Maria, who is five years old. They move from the country into the city because Shisha is a cement contractor and there are rumors that the Soviet Union will be supporting a loan for building a cement factory. Their home is located high up in the mountains, in a valley between the Hindu Kush and the mountain, something we would need to get used to is the high elevation 1,790 (meters) 5,787 (feet). Kabul is said to be 3500 years old, lies along the trade routes of South and Central Asia, and is the key location of the Ancient Silk Road. In 1955, the Soviet Union forwarded 100 million dollars in credit to Afghanistan which financed public transportation, airports and a cement factory. Shisha with his experience in the cement business was offered a good position with the factory. Their life had a promising future now for my sister, Marie and now my brother, Aslan. As

Kabul grew it became somewhat modern with even their hippie movement. A peaceful place with nice cars, young women in short dresses, friendly people building their life in their beloved Kabul. Days spent gathering under trees for tea, students at the higher Teachers College. The co-education schools, the outdoor markets with fresh fruits and vegetables, afternoon prayers were favorite things to do in the afternoon shade. Just to be together with your friends. There were so many historic events, the annual exhibition of student artwork, going to the Hotel Inter-Continental to see people from around the world and going to the Bamiyan Buddha Statue.

A second son, Breve Kahn was born on March 17, 1971 to Shisha and Shani Kahn. My father told me I was born after a very long delivery for my mother. Complications developed for the both of us. I survived but my mom died giving me life. I was damaged; I didn't have a left eye, just a scar. My mom's sister, Anita, came to live with us to take care of us. My brother and sister hated me. They blamed me for the loss of our mother. They wanted nothing to do with me. My father worked a lot, so it was just my aunt and me. She was more like my mother. She was all I had. I resented my father's love for my brother and sister and the lack of love for me. I have found memories as a young student going to outdoor class and school in mudrooms. I hated school and got into a lot of trouble with my teachers. I spent a lot of time in the mountains learning to follow the trails up and down the mountains. Soon I would know the trails better than most of the guides. I loved it. These trails were used a lot to find lost sheep or sometimes a lost tourist. I spent most of my time in the mountains. My family would say I was happier in the wild. I should go and live there.

The USSR entered neighboring Afghanistan in 1979. Afghanistan in 1979 was attempting to shore up the newly established pro-soviet regime. In Kabul, one hundred thousand Soviet soldiers took control of major cities and highways. Rebellion was swift and broad, and the Soviets dealt severely with the Mujahideen rebels and anyone who supported those leveling city villages to eliminate safe havens for their enemy. Support arrived from hundreds of groups from around the world. They were pouring in from Iran, Pakistan, China, and the United States. My city of Kabul changed with the fighting of the Mujahideen rebels. Kabul was no longer the beautiful, quiet city with all the western influence. The peace was gone. There was a power struggle between a superpower and the Afghanistan army and Mujahideen rebels. I was not going to avoid the fight but what contribution could I make and where would I make it? Would I fight for the Democratic Republic of Afghanistan with the Soviets or with Mujahideen freedom fighters' rebels standing against the loss of my beloved Kabul and Afghanistan? The Mujahideen were a dangerous option and I knew nothing about them other than they were killers and very good at it. I went to their camp and asked them to join them. They had no interest in a one-eye small man without any fighting experience. Over the next couple of months, I would follow them and find them in the mountains. They were easy to find because they were using the trail that goat herders used all the time and they were getting found by Soviets and suffered great losses. Their leader was an older man who spoke a number of languages. He was small in stature and carried his weapon, AK-47, across the front of his chest with a pistol, 45 auto and large fighting knife. He asked me in English how I was able to find them so easy. I explained that I preferred the mountains and over my life I found happiness learning the trails and caves that were short cuts or a faster route to different villages or locations on the mountain. He seemed interested. In the beginning of 1980, I was asked to lead the group of Mujahedeen as their guide. Over the next couple of years, I would learn what it took to be a guerrilla fighter. That it would take me the rest of my life to understand their beliefs and their commitment. They were from different lands. They fought not Afghanistan but their shared beliefs to honor Allah. They would gladly give their life. I would join them in their journey and beliefs. I would become a Mujahideen and would kill as many Soviets soldiers and Afghanistan soldiers to honor Allah.

THE BATTLES OF ZHAWAR

The first battle was in 1985. The Mujahedeen base at Zhawar located in Paktia Province served as a storage facility for supplies and equipment being transferred from neighboring Pakistan to supply guerrilla groups. This operation served as a training and command base. The Mujahedeen dug tunnels as far as five hundred miles into the Sadiki Guar Mountain. There was a mosque, a hotel, a medical facility, and a garage to house two T-55 tanks we captured from (DRA) Democratic Republic Afghanistan in 1983.

Our base numbered five hundred. We were armed with D-30 howitzer, BM-21 multiple rocket launchers, and ten heavy machine guns for air defense. If needed, we had other defense forces in the area to defend the base. The first attack began in September 1985 with these divisions (PF the 12th and 25th DRA) supported by Soviet air power. Our command leadership was absent. They were performing the (hajj) the pilgrimage to Mecca. The DRA forces first attacked from Khost, and succeeded in capturing the village of Bore. Northeast of Zhawar, they ran into counter forces and retreated. The main front came on September 4 and had some early success overrunning the village of Lezhi and killing one of our Commanders. We were successful stopping them at the Manway Kwando Pass. We held for ten days, and then we withdrew due to the heavy airstrikes by Soviet aircrafts. Withdrawal allowed the DRA to cross the pass and gain position to fire artillery fire at our base. We countered with two T-55 tanks and caught them by surprise. They were not expecting armored tanks. They fell back and suffered heavy losses. The DRA tried regrouping and mounting a second assault which was too late. We were reinforced by Pakistan Fighters and repelled further attacks. We fought for forty-two days. The DRA units withdrew to their base. This victory strengthened our faith and belief in our cause.

THE SECOND BATTLE

The battle offensive began February 28, 1986; this was after USSR General Secretary Mikhail Gorbachev announced his decision to withdraw Soviet troops from Afghanistan rendering Soviet units to a support role for the Afghan offensive. The DRA ground troops advanced from Khost and Gardez. Their progress was slow due to bad weather. We had successfully slowed them down with attacks to Zhawar. The main offensive was an airborne assault carried out by Afghan's 38th Command Brigade including MI-8 helicopters. Rumors circulated that when they departed on April 2 they got lost in the dark and landed on the wrong side of the Pakistani border and were captured. During the airborne assault on Zhawar with precision airstrikes by Soviet Su-25 attack aircraft, we lost some brothers in our defense. Some were trapped in caves. One hundred and fifty including one of our commanders praised Allah and escaped later even though he was targeted by a missile. They led seven-eight hundred fighters in a series of attacks against the DRA landing zones. After three days of fighting, the 38th of the DRA ceased to exist as a fighting force. We captured 530 commandos. It was reported that our leader was injured in the battle. Rumors of his death spread through the Mujahideen. Some abandoned the defense of Zhawar. The DRA forces began to overrun our defense. We are outnumbered; it seems to be 4-5 to one. Our ammunition is low. They just keep coming.

The more I kill the more of them there are. I feel a terrible pain in my left leg and then in my shoulder but still fighting then clicking out of ammo. I feel a blinding pain in my chest. Falling, I see a bright light with five images with bright gold all chanting THE CURSE OF THE RED ROSE.

BREVE KHAN KILLED IN ACTION

CHAPTER SEVEN

VIETNAM WAR TWO NAVY SEAL'S MISSIONS

April 7, 1932 Pierre and Fernanda Basin lived in the Rhone Valley in France; one of the best wine vineyards in France along with their twenty-year-old son, Victor. Victor was their only child. He was in line to take over the vineyard from his father. Victor's expertise was expanding the business, both expanding the wine making and with additional property. The vineyard offered wine tasting as a method to expand interest in the wine established by two generations of Basins and their introduction of new wines. At a wine testing gathering earlier in the year, Victor met Therese from America. She was in France on holiday. She loved France, the vineyard, our wine and my father, Victor, who fell hard for Therese, my mother. My father and mother planned a trip back to her hometown in America, in the state of Pennsylvania. It was a small town near the western New York border. The town was North East. While there, my father found what he thought was an excellent opportunity to expand the family business to America. The weather and the land of Northwestern Pennsylvania were perfect. After discussing this with his father, Pierre, my father, Victor, purchased a large crop of land and planned to move to America. Plans were made for a wedding and the move. My grandfather was concerned about my father's age, not his ability, a new wife, a new home, new business, in a new country. This is a lot for a young man to take on. The first couple of years were difficult for them. In 1935, my brother Jacques was born. The vineyard was doing very well. The winters were cold. In 1936, my brother Edouard was born. My father was excited. Unlike grandfather, he had two sons that would continue on with the family business. In 1938, my mother gave birth to twin girls, Gabrielle and Augustine.

The family was now a lot for my mother to take care of. Four young children was a full time job, something she had to do on her own. My father was working long hours, six days a week. The business grew so fast and was successful. My father would travel back to France a couple times a year to make sure things were running satisfactory in the Rhone Valley. Grandfather was getting old. His workers were loyal and had been there for a long time. My father was comfortable with how things were going. For the next twelve years both vineyards doubled in size. The Basin family had been blessed, both personally and professionally. On March 17, 1950, Augusta was born to Victor and Therese Basin. Pretty sure they weren't expecting me. I was what my brothers referred to as a mistake. I did not look like either parent. My parents were not very large babies; in fact, they all were born under seven pounds, cute, kicking and crying. Me not so much, my birth weight was eight pounds, seven ounces. Not only was I big, I had a cleft above my left eye and was not breathing when born. I needed help to breathe. It took minutes and my doctors were worried I might have gone too long without oxygen.

But the crying soon came. Life for me as a baby was lonely.

My parents hired a nanny to take care of me. They were very busy with the company or so they claimed. My siblings wanted little or nothing to do with me. I spent most of my time with Jessica, my nanny. She had a little girl, Josephine. We were the same age, and we did everything together. When we became older in high school, we started dating. Our early friendship got us through. Josephine was beautiful, and I was ugly with my scar. She took a lot of teasing from other girls in our class. Most of the boys in our class would ask Josephine out. She would tell them she was going steady with Augusta. They would respond with, "that ugly, scary kid?" I was okay in my studies at school. Josephine was very smart. We would study together, and we were in the same classes.

In the summer, we spent a lot of the time on Lake Erie. We loved the water. I asked my father if he could buy a boat. In the summer we would leave at sunup, spend all day swimming and fishing for steelhead fish. We both were like fish ourselves. One day we pulled the boat alongside a dive boat. There were a group of divers getting ready to take their deep-water dive test. We asked some questions of the guy who was in charge. He introduced himself as the Dive Master. Someone in the group yelled, "You two should join. He is the best in Erie, he was a Navy Seal." So, we did and we both loved it. The Dive Master's name was Kim. He took me under his wing as a diver, but more than that, he trained me with weapons, martial arts and endurance. We would workout at his private gym. One Saturday it was time for us to complete our Dive Master course. Both Josephine and I passed. Kim said he thought I showed promise to serve my country. I asked him "as a Seal"? He said I think you're getting a little ahead of yourself; I would have to get better in all my training. The draft was going on and Kim thought I should join the Navy and request the opportunity to try to be a Seal. My father was upset, but my number could be called and I wanted the Navy. I never wanted to work in the family business. I hated wine and the grapes that made it.

Josephine and I were in love. We were best friends and I did not want to leave her so I asked her to marry me. Josephine being Josephine at first said no, I was crushed. She claimed that at twenty, we were too young and she wanted the big wedding she dreamt about her whole life. She explained that it wasn't forever, just for now. I begged her and she was holding me and I was crying, big tough guy heading to Great Lakes boot camp.

BOOT CAMP

Arriving at Great Lakes was interesting. There were guys from everywhere, all different. We got off the bus and gathered around. We were told to line up in a straight line and reach out our right arm and touch the shoulder of the guy to your right. I was shocked on how some found this simple command hard to execute. They were too busy complaining about how they didn't want to be here but were here because they didn't want to go to the Army or Marines so they joined the Navy. Kim warned me that this was going to happen and the best thing I could do is focus on being the best recruit in the ranks. So that's what I did; no matter what it was, I would do my best. I volunteered for extra watch. I wrote home regularly. I called the cadence when we marched. I was what Kim wanted me to be and my goal was to follow in his footsteps. The day came when you could apply for a school that you would do in the Navy. I knew what I wanted and so did my Chief. He said he knew a Seal on base and it might be good to talk to him. On career day, we spoke and I told him about Kim. It turns out they knew each other and he thought I would make a great candidate. I should request training on the West Coast. I did and was accepted. Graduation was Friday and I could invite my family but they were all too busy. My Josephine was coming. A lot of the guys would rag me about my blind girlfriend. How else could she see anything in me. I was so proud to have her there. She looked beautiful. She met a couple of guys but most of them had orders and were heading for leave at home, then to their duty station or school. We were heading back home. I had two weeks' leave and I would spend most of it begging Josephine to marry me. "I am not saying no forever but no for now."

NAVAL AMPHIBIOUS BASE CORONADO

I was ordered to Coronado in January 1944. Coronado is a shore base for operations, training, for amphibian units on the west coast. The base is approximately 1000 acres (four square kilometers) including a main base, training beaches, recreational marina, enlisted housing and a state park. The base has both an ocean and bay side. Most of the bay side consists of fill dredged from San Diego Bay in the early 1940s. When I arrived, I was both excited and a little intimidated. Kim told me what to expect and to focus on one day at a time. He said there would be days when you can only focus one moment at a time. This would be the most difficult physical and mental challenge to see if you have what it takes to be a Seal. Most do not. It will take every ounce of determination to not ring the bell or wash out. You have been training hard; you prepared your body for this challenge. Your mind will drain your fatigue both physically and mental. The training will attack both and test you to see how you react under the worst pressure, from no sleep and pain. It attacks everyone the same. Not everyone reacts the same. The last weeks have been the single most difficult time in my life. I thought I was in great shape, but it wasn't enough. On the runs I never finished in the front, always in the middle. I was average, except when it came to swimming. I was always at the top and my swim buddy hated it because he had to keep up. Sometimes I had to slow down a bit, not a lot. I can thank Lake Erie for my swimming success.

VIETNAM WAR

During the Vietnam War, the newly created Seal teams were initially tasked with training indigenous South Vietnamese forces to operate as maritime commandos. Later in the war, twelve-man Seal platoons rotated in and out of deployment in South Vietnam with their battle skills and launched their reputation as an elite special operation force. They operated at night deploying from boats and helicopters to carry out short direct-action missions like ambushes, hit and run raids, personnel recovery intelligence, and collections and reconnaissance patrols. The Viet Cong dubbed the fearsome Seals the "MEN WITH GREEN FACES" for the camouflage face paint they favored.

My first order in Vietnam I was to report to U.S. Naval Riverine Forces under the command of Naval Forces Vietnam Task Force 116. The Navy's river patrol operation

developed largely in response to the defi-
ciencies of the Vietnam Navy. Most of the
Navy riverboats were deployed as ferries and
re-supply the Army of the Republic of
Vietnam (ARV) units rather than to deny the
enemy the use of South Vietnam's rivers.
The Mekong Delta alone contained over
3,000 miles of waterways. If the 116 were expected to defeat the insurgency, they needed
to establish a presence in the brown water.
They established 120 boats. The U.S. Navy
River Patrol Force, called Task Force-116,
was established in December 1965 to assist
in patrolling the main rivers of the Mekong
Delta plus the shipping channel running
through the Rung Sat Swamp. The Navy
adapted a commercially built thirty-one-foot
long fiberglass pleasure boat for river patrol.
Replacing screws with water jets and adding
machine guns for armament. We were catching a ride up river to Ben Tre on the Ham
River, a city of about 75,000 and the capital
of Kian Hoe Province. Our Mission was to
provide surveillance. There was some intelligence advising of a lot of Viet Cong troop
movements. The swift boat dropped our
team about six clicks south of Ben Tre where
we gear up, apply our green paint, and move

out. We traveled two clicks and came to what our Intel told us was a trail. What we were seeing was more like a road. We didn't see any troop movement, so we moved back into the jungle for our radioman to call into Command to report what we found. Now we were ordered to take cover for surveillance, for movement overnight and move out at first light. Dark turned into black; we were under a dark moon so vision was difficult. We spread out fifty yards apart with a staggered formation. At 01:30 A.M., we started hearing light foot traffic, a hell of a lot of it. What was concerning was that the movement was to our south moving toward Ben Tre. Chief orders us to close ranks. We cut our distance from fifty yards to twenty yards. The problem was the swift boats were two clicks right into the strength of the VC. A lot of time the VC did not want to fight. We may be able to quietly get past them. We were having success. We made one click south. The sundown was in thirty minutes; we rallied but decided no way we would make our extraction point. We would hold here and hope to get a message to swift boat Petty Officer to delay time until 03:30 A.M. Now we were hearing movement. We buried it. We feared the worst; the VC was hugging us. This was a tactical move. When they fought, they moved slowly in, close inside heavy weapons. Soon we would be in close contact with the VC. Our cover was good so we expected to let them in close and wait until they were in the kill zone. We were still staggered boot to helmet; twenty yards abreast it will require K bars and forty-fives on our bellies. Waiting one minute nothing; the next a VC almost steps on my head. He doesn't see me. I wait until he gets just past me, now I am up, K bar up in my left-hand right hand over his mouth. K Bar across his neck. The sharp knife goes deep, damn near cut his head off. He grabs at my hand to scream, just muffled, gargled sound. I hold on a little longer, lowering him down. My teammates have similar results. The Chief had one down and was engaged with another. He guts him. We go quietly. It seems like hours and nothing. Chief decides our plan is to crawl deeper into the jungle; then south to the extraction point. It took time to belly crawl. We were at the extraction point. We are going to swim to the swift boat in the middle of the river. This river is not very deep, but it has different depths. At some point, we would be exposed. The swift boat could cover if needed. They did not want to because there was a lot of VC in the area. We walked some and swam very little but we all made it to the boat. The rest of the tour, our team was working on the rivers with small hit and run raids, a lot of extractions of Army Special Forces, and surveillance. The team works well together. In January, I had leave to go back to the world. I already re-enlisted another four years. I arrived at Pittsburgh International Airport. While picking up my luggage, some kid walked up to me, called me baby killer, and spat on my uniform. I was shocked. I wanted to punch him in the face or worse. I had seen a lot of my brothers killed or injured in Vietnam. I just walked away. They told us not to wear our uniform but I did not have civilian clothes that fit, I had lost thirty pounds. I wore my dress blues. I love that uniform. I am to meet Josephine in Pittsburgh. I want to take her to a nice place for dinner and ask her to marry me. She is going to pick me up outside the airport. When I walk out, I see my father and I ask him did something happen to Josephine? Is she ok? He gave me a hug and a kiss and said,

"No she is fine. She could not come because she was upset that you re-enlisted in the Navy. She does not want that life. She just could not face you. She still loves you but cannot be with you." I was upset but as I wrote to her, I can't leave the team or the Navy. I called, even drove by her house. She wouldn't see me. I wanted to see her before I left. I had orders to Subic Bay to the amphibious-transport submarine.

MISSION

We put underway. The mission was to be off the coast of North Vietnam on a rescue mission for two U.S. pilots hiding from VC. The plan was for us to leave at night from the submerged submarine in a swimmer delivery vehicle (SDV) piloted by two UDT-11 operators and head for a small island off the mouth of the Red River. We decided to conduct a clandestine reconnaissance mission that night. Shortly after midnight, our team launched from the submarine. The strong currents took us off course. After one hour, we aborted the mission. We could not locate our submarine. We scuttled our underpowered SDV after its battery power was gone.

At sunup, we rescued a few miles off the coast. The team was flown back to the command ship. At 2400 hours, the team was to be transported back to submarine by helicopter. We were to perform a night water drop next to the submarine. During the briefing with the pilots, the Chief and Chief Warren Officer (CWO) went over the maximum limits for the drop. We were 20/20 feet of altitude at airspeed of twenty knots or an equivalent combination. When the helicopter arrived near the submarine's expected position, we could not locate the submarine. The pilots desperately searched for the submarine beacon. The team prepared to enter the water and lock into the submerged submarine. I was first out. The chief was yelling at (CWO). He was convinced we were too high and too fast. We were dealing with high waves and heavy winds. The pilots were insisting we go, as soon as I left the door I knew. I hit so hard I heard my neck break, and there was a bright light, six figures chanting THE CURSE OF THE RED ROSE and shining red and gold metal.

PETTY OFFICER SECOND CLASS

AUGUSTA BASIN KILLED ON
MAY 21, 1972

CHAPTER EIGHT

CHINA-SOVIET UNION AVOIDED WORLD WAR III

Jamba (Jahm-pah), meaning loving kindness (Tibetan name for the Buddha Mairea) and his wife Norbie (nor-boo) (Meaning Jewel) live in Tibet, in Haydon the prefecture part of Qinghai province. We were happy living on a small farm that was in my family for generations. My wife and I farmed our land to sell in local markets along with our own use. I was also in the Tibetan Army. I would go when needed for local skirmish or invasions from other border countries. We were newly married and learning about each other, farming, and my military service.

Recently I have been called away due to border conflicts with both China and India. The Khampas Tibetans who live here were fiercely independent. The Lhasa Tibetan held each other in mutual contempt and dislike. The Khampas in some cases hating Lhasa rule even more than Chinese rule. This was why the Khampas did little to resist Chinese forces as they entered eastern Kham and subsequently took over all of Tibet. After months of failed negotiations, there were attempts by Lhasa to secure forging support and assistance and troop build ups by the People's Republic of China (PRC) and Tibet. The People's Liberation Army (PLA) crossed the Jinsha River on October 6 or 7, 1950 into Lhasa-controlled Chamdo, crossing the defector border at five locations. Two PLA units surrounded and outnumbered our forces. They captured the border town of Chamdo on October 19. By that time, 114 PLA soldiers and 180 Tibetan soldiers had been killed or wounded. The Chamdo Governor and the Commander of our forces, Ngubo Gnawing Jigme, surrendered with his 2700 men. Shang Guohua claimed 5738 enemy troops were liquidated and 5700 destroyed, and more than 3000 peacefully surrendered after confiscating our weapons. The PLA soldiers gave us lectures on socialism and a small amount of money before allowing us to return home. According to our leader, the Dalai Lama of the PLA did not attack civilians. After the Battle of Chamdo and the incorporation of Tibet into the People's Republic of China, the Tibetan Army kept its remaining force. I would spend my next eighteen years serving in the PLA, gaining rank, and accepting my commission as officer on December 7, 1968. My lovely wife, Norbie and my son, Qiqng (Meaning stronger better) were still farming our little farm in Tibet. I did well in PLA. I believe I would have done better if not for my hideous scar above my eye and my deformed forehead. This is all people see when they look at me.

HOW THE SOVIET UNION AND CHINA ALMOST STARTED WORLD WAR III

In March 1969, a unit of the People's Liberation Army (PLA) raided A Soviet border outpost on Shembo Island, killing two units and injuring countless more Russian soldiers. This incident brought Russia and China to the brink of war; this conflict could lead to the use of nuclear weapons being used by both sides. After two weeks of clashes, the conflict diminished. In the immediate wake of the conflict, both the USSR and China prepared for war with the Red Army redeploying to the far east and the PLA into full mobilization. The Soviets enjoyed an overwhelming technological advantage over China in 1969. Beijing had constructed the largest Army in the World with the majority mustered within reach of the Sino-Soviet border. The Russian Red Army concentrated its strength in Eastern Europe to prepare for a conflict with NATO. The Chinese would claim conventional superiority along the border. China's manpower advantage wouldn't mean that the PLA could advance into the USSR. What the Chinese had in manpower they lacked in air power and logistics to seize a large part of Soviet Territory. The other obstacle was that the long Sino-Soviet border would be enough time for a Soviet response by redeploying from the East. A NATO attack was not likely, allowing the Soviets to attack XINJIANG and points west the first round of Sino-Soviet hostilities.

I was leading our patrol. On March 2, the fight on Shembo Island we marched over the frozen Usury River, which is the boundary between China and the Soviet Union. We engaged the Soviets before marching toward the Island and the Soviet border guard post located on the bank of the river. The Soviets were coming to meet us on the Island, and this was not the first time we did this. It has always been disputed whose island it was, most of the time it would end up in fist fights or club beatings with shouting demanding to leave using fire hoses. My orders were different today when the Soviets were in range. I was to open up with automatic weapon fire as we engaged them. We killed their officer and six of their men before they knew what hit them. We were under fire for two hours, killing thirty-one Soviets and wounding fourteen. We took some casualties. The number is classified.

THE SECOND ROUND OF SINO-SOVIET HOSTILITIES

Thirteen days later they were again heading for a confrontation with Soviets on Shembo, this time with a larger force and a lot more firepower. The month we spent fighting we would fight several more battles along the border. The battles were mainly with machine gun fire. We launched an attack with six men patrolling at night along the border mostly for surveillance. Our mission was not to engage. We had been here almost thirty days and there were some intense battles but not a lot. We thought the Soviets might be withdrawing so we needed intelligence on where and if they were in the process of withdrawing. We advanced without any resistance. We are advancing slowly when the machine gun fire breaks out to our right and left flank. I lost two men instantly. With limited cover on the bank of the river, we are a slight grade to the tree level where there is some cover. We started out with a belly crawl and started up the grade. We can see machine gun fire overhead. We were completely pinned down. If we retreat, the machine gun will cut us to pieces. Our only chance is to move forward to close the distance on their weapons and attack. We check our ammo and begin to move up and forward. The soldier to my right tries to lift up to lob a grenade the gun cuts him in half. The machine gun stops. We knew the Soviets were advancing; we needed to get to the top of the bank and fight on even ground otherwise they would have the advantage and we would be dead. We fixed bayonets and charged up the remaining bank. When we crested the bank, my men were killed with small arms fire. I was able to kill the first soldier with a bayonet. There was a pain in my head. I see seven shadows, all with my scar, all chanting THE CURSE OF THE RED ROSE. I also see a brilliant gold medal and something red.

Jamba was killed in action March 29, 1969 with a gunshot to his head.

CHAPTER NINE

BLOOD DIAMONDS

Sierra Leone is a country in western Africa. The country name comes from a fifteenth century Portuguese explorer, Pedro de Sentra, the first European to map Freetown Harbor then sign it. The original Portuguese name, Sierra Leone "Lion Mountain" referred to the hills that surrounded the harbor. The capital, Freetown, is one of the world's largest natural harbors. Most of the Sierra Leone population engaged in subsistence agriculture. Sierra Leone is a mining center; its land yields diamonds, gold, bauxite and rutile (titanium dioxide). The fact that the abundance of this exists in Sierra Leone created internal conflicts and destroyed the country from late 1980 onward, culminating in a brutal civil war from 1991 to 2002. Since the end of the war, Sierra Leone underwent the difficult task of rebuilding. Seven years after the war hundreds of children and youth are exploited daily. They labor in open pit diamond mines.

Jawed and Gerorigieia live with their

three children. Abdul first son, Aiah second son, and Marajo their daughter. They are subsistence farmers; they all work in the fields, even the three-year-old Marajo. The crop yield is very low, and my family is starving. Our home is a four-wall block building with no roof. I am praying that farming would take care of my family. I must find diamonds. For days I am standing calf deep in muddy brown water here at the mine where I work. I finally found the first stone in days. I can expect a little more than a dollar for it. Hardly seems worth it. This is my only hope. Sierra Leone is a bloody affair, in which diamonds played a starring role. The vilified forging mine owners and local elites with a firm grip on the industry's profits. The losers here are the miners like me in the Kono District. We work for little or no pay hoping to become rich. We mine the majority of Sierra Leone diamonds by hand from alluvial deposits near the surface. Anyone who has a shovel bucket and sieve is in business. In a country with few formal jobs there are 150,000 diggers trying to survive. I report to the mine to face the routine of mining with about 300 diggers sifting through tons of gravel. Our mine is divided into 300 square yards each under the control of the license holder who must be a Sierra Leonean; it's the law. I find that a lot of the time they are nothing but fronts for foreign backers or migrants from the Middle East or other African countries. Some of the diggers are paid a small sum per day, about seventy-five cents and are provided tools, food and shelter. This is about 30 percent of whatever their backers claim the value of the diamonds they find. Other workers have no interest in their find and are paid two dollars per day. Still others, like me, work for a share of the gravel they extract from the watery pits. In my arrangement, I shoulder most of the risk and the loss. With not having any success at the mine, backers tell me about a village about ninety miles from the mine where diggers are finding Diamonds. I talk it over with my wife and decide to travel to the village.

When I arrived, it was a village but now it's an open landscape that is pockmarked with holes the size of water wells. Holes that a man can barely squeeze into. I arrived at daybreak with my simple tools, an old pick, a simple rope and a torn sack. I met a five-man team. They have no shoes, flashlights, hard hats, or even gloves. I manage to make it down into the well. The shaft is deep, dark, cold and very dangerous. The walls are loose, accidents happen; many miners have been buried alive. I need to keep digging for my hungry family. It's terrible work all I do is work morning to evening and come up empty. I cannot think of a worse way to make a living. Most diggers have no choice but to work. It is hard to find anything and they are tired of fighting in the various militias that roam these badlands. These men and boys want to make an honest living. After months of climbing up and down the tiny little holes getting stuck many times, living through cave-ins, and working sunup to sundown, I bring home, after paying expenses, less than fifty dollars. What will I do? How can I support my family? Some of my team are talking about going to the militias. They claim they make more fighting. I have to do something, if not an honest living I will do what it takes. I start back home when we come upon a village, there are bodies everywhere with the ears and the arms and legs cut off. Women and young girls are crying, screaming, babies lying dead or multitudes of women telling stories of horrible rapes. Their bodies mutilated. I am sick and frightened. I think of my own village and my family. I go and try to help a little girl who has blood all over her and her mother is trying to console her. She screams and points to me. Her mother said the man who did this to her had a scar like mine above his left eye and he looked like me. I wondered what type of man could do this to a little girl. I asked the men with me if they knew and they claimed it was rebel forces and civilian militias. I swear I will do whatever to protect villages from these savage actions.

VIOLENCE

Diamond mining is violent from killing, to sexual, to torture most of the time by rebel groups but also by mining companies and governments in Africa's diamond fields. Conflict diamonds or blood diamonds are rough diamonds mined in conflict areas that are used by armed thugs to pay for conflict and human rights abuses. Conflict diamonds originated from Sierra Leone among other places. The volume of conflict diamonds has been said to be between 4 percent and 15 percent of the world trade of rough diamonds somewhere in the range of 7.9 billion in trade in one year, enough to purchase many weapons. The sale of diamonds is what is fueling the conflict in Sierra Leone, Liberia, Angola, and Democratic Republic of the Congo (DRC) estimating some three million people in wars have died. In Sierra Leone, an estimated 50,000 were killed. Rebels chopped off the hands and feet of women, children, and men in the desire to frighten civilians away from the alluvial diamond fields. Diamonds are to be a symbol of love, commitment, and a joyful union of loving couples. For the many in diamond enriched countries these beautiful stones are nothing more than a curse rather than a blessing more often than not they produce war and violence.

THE WAR

After we leave the village, we head toward our village some twenty-three miles away. I am so worried about my family I can think of nothing else. As we cross over a small creek, we come up on a unit of the Sierra Leone army; they advise us they are tracking the Rebels who attacked the village we just left. The commanders see how upset I am, and I have so many questions about who they are and how can anyone be so inhumane to do this. I am told this is going on in the entire country and he is having trouble keeping his men because of their concern for their own families. He asks if I would like to join them as they are heading to another village. I talked to the men who were with me. They decided they were not interested and wanted to return to the village to check on their families. I can't imagine the little girl pointing at me so afraid of not only what happened to her but of me. I must try and stop these brutal sick animals. I agree to join them as a civilian. I asked the commander how far to the next village. He said about ten miles or less. The village is the home of the men that were traveling with me, so I am praying that the rebels don't beat us there. As we get close, we see smoke, not a good sign; as we enter the village from the south, we are met by women running toward us covered in blood screaming and begging for help. We leave our medic with the women and move into the village. What we see is beyond our imagination. In the streets are a pile of bodies with blood everywhere, bodies missing arms and heads of both women and children. We go into a home, lying on the floor are five women lying on their backs with their feet cut off and are naked, sexually mutilated. They are bleeding; it seems there is blood everywhere standing in puddling blood. I look for the men that I knew that I mined diamonds with. I can't find them anywhere. I ask a woman sitting on the trail and she points down the trail. I start down the trail; I am running now, and I see where the smoke is coming from. I found the men; they were in piles now burning, and some weren't dead. They were screaming about their sons and the Rebels took them. I raise my rifle and shoot and kill the men who are suffering while burning alive. The commander comes running toward me wondering what I am shooting at when he sees he fires his weapon as well. When we finish, we look at the fire, tears are running down both of our faces; the smell and sight is unbelievable.

My rage is out of control. My fear is my village and my family would be next. I ask the commander what he found out about who did this. He was told by dying women it was two different Rebel groups. Apparently the one group that killed the people in the other village and another group joined in here. There are over twenty men and young boys taken from both villages heading for the next one. I want to go after them. They are not that far in front of us; they only left the village an hour ago so we could catch up to them. We need to leave now. The commander doesn't want to follow them now. We were outnumbered, and he wanted to wait until tomorrow for reinforcements to get here. I told him I believe my village is only a couple of miles from here. If we wait until tomorrow these animals will kill my family and destroy my village. I have to get there please; the commander helps me save them. The commander agrees to help so we leave three men at the village along with our medic who was trying to save lives. We are a unit of eleven Sierra Leone army and me going against twenty plus cold-blooded killers. We move fast, running what we see motivates us to move without stopping. We have to get there first to prevent this from happening again. As we are getting close to my village, I hear weapons fire. We keep moving. As we enter the village, we encounter five rebels. We kill all five and keep moving through the village. We come upon two rebels raping a young woman and we kill the both of them. Seven rebels are leading the men and boys out of the village toward our farming fields. We can't get a position to fire without killing the men from the village so we spread out a flank to the field hoping we can get a better position there. When they arrive, they line up the villagers. They are going to execute them. We have to move to a better firing position. We killed five of the seven. The other two start shooting at the villagers and they kill four before we can kill them, all young boys. We free them. Men tell us the rest of the rebels are in their homes killing and raping the women and young girls. We give the seven weapons to the men that had some experience with weapons; they advise what we thought were two rebel groups are three. I told my commander I was going to my home to save my family. As I arrive, I see my sons lying in front of my home. I see my two boys being held by three rebels. I shoot the first one in the head and when I turn on the other two, he drops his AK-47 and runs. I shoot the third one. I make sure my sons are ok. I move into my home. The first I see is my wife huddling in the corner holding our baby. She is naked and covered in blood. My baby is crying, my wife rolls over, and there is blood all over her chest; her breast has been cut off. I see movement to my right. I return a fire. There are four rebels and I kill two of them. The other two rush me and knock my weapon out of my hand. The one to my left drives a bloody knife in my chest the second drives his in my shoulder. I grab the knife out of my chest and drive into his throat. I rip it out just as the second rebel drives his knife deep into my chest. At the same time, I plunge my knife deep in his chest and we both fall. As I am falling, I re-move the knife from my chest and drive into his back. My wife screams, my baby cries. I see eight soldiers chanting THE CURSE OF THE RED ROSE. I see a bright light and a gold and red shining medal.

CHAPTER TEN

HALABJA CHEMICAL ATTACK

The Peshmerga have historically been Kurdish guerrilla forces combating the ruling power in the area of Iraqi Kurdistan. My name is Kardox, a leader in the Kurdish guerrilla army and I fight for Peshmerga. The word Peshmerga is from the time of the Sasanian Empire, the last Persian Empire before the rise of Islam. One of the leading powers of its time (224 AD through 651 AD) they were known best for their military power, best troops, and the use of heavy armored cavalry. The top units were Gyan-avspar Peshmerga, meaning "those who sacrifice their lives".

FIRST IRAQI–KURDISH WAR (1961-1970)

September 1961 Kurdish leader Mustafa Barazni revolted against Baghdad authority, He started with 600 followers by the spring 1962 had risen to 5000 full-timed guerrillas and another 5000-15000 to be called up to help if needed. When he attacked in autumn 1961, he caught Iraqi government forces, principally the 2nd Division, unprepared. A counterattack by the 2nd Division was able to reverse most of the Kurdish gains before Barzani forces were compelled to withdraw into the mountains during the winter of 1961-1962.

SECOND IRAQI-KURDISH WAR (1974-1975)

Secret negotiations between Barzani and Saddam Hussein led to the "March Manifesto". The agreement included a pledge from the Kurds to stop their rebellion, and in exchange the regime would allow the establishment of a Kurdish autonomous region in areas where the Kurds were a majority. The agreement was to be implemented within four years. However, during those four years the regime encouraged the "Arabization" of the oil rich Kurdish areas. After decreasing the number of Kurds in the North for four years, the regime demanded the implementation of the manifesto. The Kurds weren't willing to implement it. After the ultimatum extended by the Ba'ath regime expired, the manifesto became a law on March 11, 1974. Clashes between the rebels and the Iraqi security forces erupted immediately. The fighting cost the lives of ten thousand Iraqi soldiers. With the help of Iran's continued assistance to the rebels, the Iraqi Army was unable to crush the rebellion. Tehran even deployed two divisions of the Iranian Army inside Iraq in January 1975. Saddam Hussein, having committed to confrontation with the Kurds, was determined not to lose the fight. In 1974 he began negotiations with the Iranian Shah Mohammad Reza Pahlavi. An agreement was reached and signed by the sides during an OPEC summit in Algiers. The Agreement guaranteed that Iran would stop assisting the Kurdish rebels.

IRAN-IRAQ WAR 1980-1988

The Peshmerga rebels sided with Iran against Iraq. The Peshmerga's support to Iran was a very important element in Iran's early success on the Northern Front (Iraqi Kurdistan) this coalition led to several successful Iranian military offensives; they still were unable to gain control of any cities or towns of significance. The Iraqi military responded to the Peshmerga rebels by launching various military campaigns against them and ultimately employed the use of chemical weaponry which leads to military success against the Peshmerga however this claimed the lives of almost 100.000 Kurds.

HALABJA CHEMICAL ATTACK

I was in charge of a unit of sixteen men stationed outside the city of Halabja. We were defending the Iraqi attempt to repel the Iranian operation. I felt we could engage and stop their advance; we have success not losing cities. It was March 16, 1988; it was a beautiful spring day. We arrived in the city of Halabja at 1200 noon. I was leading my men and came upon people walking around.

We encountered no resistance. A little girl ran up to me and screamed when she saw the scar on my face and ran back to her mother. I had a strange feeling in my stomach, and I felt something wasn't right. Within minutes artillery was falling all around us, a direct hit on my unit, nine of my men blown to bits. We had planes overhead dropping bombs on the town. We were in the Northern neighborhoods which is where the bombing is concentrated. We looked for cover and found some in the basement of a large building at 14:00. The bombing slowed when we began moving out from our cover. I wasn't sure what we were hearing. It sounded like a medal falling and heard sounds like bombs falling. Two of my men started yelling "GAS". We got to our trucks and closed the windows and started moving. All I could hear was the sound of us running over the dead bodies of innocent people. We saw people lying on the ground, vomiting a green liquid, others acting hysterical before falling on the ground lying motionless. I smell an aroma that reminds me of apples. My driver starts vomiting green liquid all over the windshield. Then the truck hits a car in the street. I am engulfed with a horrible ugly smell like rotting garbage, then the smell of apples, then eggs. I look out to see hundreds of dead bodies scattered all around us. I begin to laugh hysterically before I see nine images all saying the Curse of the Red Rose. I see a shining gold shield with something in the middle. Kardox died of a chemical attack which killed between 3,000 and 5,000 people and injured 7,000 to 10,000, most of them civilians. An eyewitness spoke of Iraqi aircraft, coordinated by helicopters conducted up to fourteen bombings with seven planes in each and told us of clouds of white, black, and yellow smoke rising above of the city about fifty meters in the air.

Kradox dies March 16, 1988

MEDICAL

Iranian physicians reported that victims of the chemical attacks on Halabja showed signs and symptoms of Cyanide Poisoning and substantial quantities of Mustard Gas and others. Survivors said the gas at first smelled of sweet apples and reported people died in a number of ways, suggesting a combination of toxic chemicals. Some of the victims just dropped dead while others died laughing, while still others suffered and it took time to die, fist burning and blistering or coughing up green vomit. Many were killed in the panic that followed the attack especially those who were blinded by the chemicals

CHAPTER ELEVEN

BATTLE OF NASSAU

The Continental Navy was the Navy of the United States during the American Revolution War, and was formed in 1775. The Continental Navy's patron was John Adams. The goal of the Navy was to intercept shipments of the British materials and disrupt British maritime commercial operations. The fleet was made up of converted merchantmen because of no funding.

On June 12, 1775, the Rhode Island General Assembly established a Navy for the colony of Rhode Island. The creation of a Continental Navy came from Rhode Island because its merchants' widespread shipping activities were harassed by British frigates. On August 26, 1775, Rhode Island General Assembly passed a resolution that there be a Single Continental fleet funded by the Continental Congress. The resolution was introduced in the Continental Congress on October 3, 1775 but was tabled. George Washington began to acquire ships, starting with the schooner, Hannah, which was chartered by Washington from the Merchant and Continental Army. Hannah was commissioned at sea September 5, 1775 out of the port of Beverly Massachusetts. The United States Navy recognizes October 13, 1775 as the official date of Establishment. On this day, Congress authorized the purchase of two vessels to be armed for cruise against British merchants. The ships were Andrew Doria and Cabot. The first ship in commission was the USS Alfred which was purchased November 4, 1775. On November 10, 1775 the Continental Congress passed a resolution calling for two battalions of Marines to serve in the fleet. The USS Alfred was commissioned December 3, 1775. John Adams drafted its first governing regulations which were adopted by Congress on November 28, 1775 and remained in effect throughout the Revolutionary War. The Rhode Island resolution by the Continental Congress passed December 13, 1775, authorizing the construction of thirteen frigates in the next three months: five with thirty-two guns, five with twenty-eight guns and three with twenty-four guns.

Alfred, a 450-ton rigged vessel originally named Black Prince. She was built in Philadelphia in 1774. No builder survived. It is thought that John Wharton may have built her while we operated under the flag of Continental Navy as a merchant ship. The Black Prince is named after Edward the Black Prince and launched in 1774. The Continental Navy of what became the United States acquired her in 1775, renamed her Alfred after the ninth century old English monarch Alfred the Great, and commissioned her as a warship. I served as a Quartermaster LT Richard Clark. I served on merchant ships most of my life sailing from Philadelphia and London. Life at sea suits me. I love sailing on the open seas. My mates like to say I was born to be a man of the Sea with my eye patch and forehead scar. The only thing missing would be a hook for a hand and a peg leg. John Berry served as the only Master during his career as a

Philadelphia merchantman. We launched in the autumn 1774, while relations between the Colonies and England grew tense. The ship was fitted out quickly so that we could load and sail for Bristol on the last day of 1774; we would not return until the spring of 1775. Rumors were that the American commerce would be interrupted. Our owners wanted to export cargo to England. We raced to load a provision. We sailed on May 7, bound for London. We did not arrive until June 27. We set sail from the Thames River on August 10. We encountered contrary winds during our westward voyage and arrived in Philadelphia on October 4. While we were aboard, the conflict between America and England grew more intense. More colonies acting in Congress supported Massachusetts for the quest for freedom. George Washington is now in command of the American Army and had besieged British occupied Boston. Correspondence with the Black Prince was brought back from England to members of the Continental Congress reporting that the British Government was sending to America un-armed ships heavily supplied with gunpowder and arms. The intelligence re-

sulted in Congress on October 13 to author-
ize the fitting of two American warships with
ten guns each to capture the ships and supply
the weapons and gunpowder to
Washington's army, who were running out
of supplies. Congress also decided on
October 30 to add two more ships to the
American Navy, one having twenty Guns
and the other larger, but not larger than
thirty-six guns. My ship the Black Prince was
the larger ship. The Navy purchased Black
Prince on November 4, 1775, renamed her
Alfred four days later, and ordered her fitted
out as a man of war. Our ship was placed in
commission on December 3, 1775 with
Capt. Dudley Saltonstall in command and
LT Richard Clark at the helm. Four other
vessels joined us in the Continental Navy,
Columbus, Cabot, Andrew dories and the
Providence. On January 4, 1776 a cold snap
froze the river and the bay, stopping our progress at Reedy Island for some six weeks. A
warmup allowed us free from the ice in
February. We sailed for our first operation
and the Marines American First amphibious
operation. Our captain issued a proclamation, which promised not to harm "the
people or property of New Providence "if

they did not resist. The following day the Governor, Montfort Browne, surrendered Fort Nassau after all or most of the gunpowder had been moved to St Augustine. Before setting sail, we removed the guns and ordnance. We led the Americans fleet homeward out of Nassau Harbor. On St. Patrick's Day we captured a six-gun schooner ship and an eight-gun ship. At midnight, we encountered a twenty-gun ship during the battle from the British frigate and cut our tiller line rendering Alfred unable to maneuver or pursue. The rest of the fleet chased the frigate, but she disappeared over the horizon when we reached New London, Rhode Island. Many of the Officers of the Fleet were complaining about our Commander and later he was relieved of command.

We were inactive throughout the summer mainly because of funding. There were just no funds and a shortage of men. In August our first lieutenant on our cruise to New Providence who helped to fit Alfred as a warship was placed in command, Captain John Paul Jones We arrived in the waters off Cape Breton with the sloop Providence sailing with us. We took three prizes: the Brigantine Active, the armed transport MELLISH and the Snow Kitty. Providence developed leaks and sailed for home; we continued our cruise alone. Two days later we captured three colliers off Louisburg bound for New York with coal for the British Army and on November 26, captured the ten-gun Letter of Marque John of Liverpool. On the homeward voyage, we were pursued by HMS Milford. We were able to escape after a four-hour chase. We arrived at Boston on December 19 and began a major refit. Our new captain was Elisha Henman in May 1777, but we did not get underway until August 22 when we sailed to France with Raleigh to obtain military supplies. We arrived in Orient on October 6 and set sail for home on December 29. Our course was around the coast of Africa where we captured a small sloop then set a heading for West Indies with hopes to add to our score before heading northward for home. We encountered a British warship and we attempted to flee but we were not able to outrun the faster bigger ship. The warship caught us and began firing their guns. We were hit and dead in the water. The Captain hailed us and demanded us to surrender. Our captain refused. They were coming in closer. We fought for what seemed forever; the warship had too many guns and we were losing men. The ship was dead in the water and we lost all ability to sail, our masts were damaged, our tiller ropes were cut, our guns were doing little damage to the warship. I turned to the Captain to see what to do and felt a crushing blow to my back. I saw a bright light with a group of what looked like soldiers and a gold shield all chanting THE CURSE OF THE RED ROSE.

LT Richard Clark killed March 1778.

CHAPTER TWELVE

COLOMBIAN WAR ON DRUGS

We live on a coffee farm in Cali, Colombia that my mother's family has owned for over a hundred and fifty years. We live as kin groups which are large families living together to work and farm the fields. My Name is Simon. I live with my father Fernando, my mother Maria, my brothers Alexander and Edgar Gomez, my mother's parents, and her four brothers and their families all toll twenty-six people. I am the oldest of the children and have the responsibility to manage the children working the fields. My days are long, and I wake up before sunup and work to sundown. We begin each day at breakfast. Our day is broken up by school work taught by my mother and my aunts. The education is hard and my mother is very tough. After school, we return to the fields to work. My mother works right alongside my father, as do the wives of her brothers. We are proud of our coffee and expect the best coffee in Colombia. Our farm is located in the Valle del Cauca Cal, we grow Colombia "Excelso" coffee. Excelso is a grading term for exportable coffee from Colombia not related to the variety of cupping profiles. EP (European Preparation) specifies that the raw beans are all hand sorted to remove any defective beans and foreign material. Excelso coffee beans are large, but slightly smaller than Supremo coffee beans. Excelso beans are screen size of 15-16, versus Supremo beans, which are sized on screen size of seventeen. Supremo and Excelso coffee beans can be harvested from the same tree, but are sorted by size. Excelso accounts for the greatest volume of coffee exported from Colombia. Excelso beans are harvested from a variety of regions in the Valle del Cauca at about 13 percent of the total production.

I will be finishing school with my teachers next month. My mother and father want me to attend college. They believe college would help them with the farm and our family business. I would prefer to stay on the farm and continue my work and not attend more school and don't see how any more book learning will help the farm. My brother, Alexander, is the age I was when I started managing the fields so my parents feel he is ready to take over my duties and I would be free to attend college. My parents have always protected me. I was not allowed to play in sports or ride horses because of my birth defect. I was born with limited use of my left eye because of a scar on my forehead and eyelid. I hate that my parents treat me like I am made of glass and will break. My mother encouraged me to go because she says good students should go to college. I don't think that is the reason. There is a lot of trouble in Colombia and she is trying to protect me. I will honor my parents' wishes and do what is expected of me. In the fall I will be attending the University of Antioquia located in Medellin Colombia. The oldest departmental University in Colombia founded in 1803 by A royal Decree issued by King Charles IV of Spain under the name Franciscan college (Spanish: Colegio de Franciscanos) it is considered one of Colombia's best universities and one of the best medical schools in Colombia. My six years at university was the best time of my life. The studies were difficult and required a lot of study. My parents demanded my grades reflected on the family and expected hard work and dedication. I learned that I was not glass and would not break. I was as tough as anyone with two good eyes and proved myself by playing football. I don't think my mother ever really approved but she would come to matches and cheer. In May 1973, I graduated with a degree in medicine. The happiest day in my life. My parents and my whole family were there and were excited about having a doctor in the house. I kept telling them that was a way off yet, but it didn't matter they knew it would happen.

When I returned home, I spoke to my father because he looked so much older than when I left. We spoke about the farm and how it was going, and it was always the same answer: everything fine, nothing to concern you. You could not be Colombian and ignore the drug cartels killing and the amount of corruption everywhere. A lot of farmers stopped farming coffee and started in planting for the drug cartels. He would say we are losing our way as a country we must do something. Our farm has been in our family forever. We are good religious people. The temptation of so much money was taking its toll on him and he was getting pressure from my mother and brothers. I decided I would not let my father fight this fight alone. I am going to do something about it, a fight for Colombia and my family.

SOME OF THE HISTORY OF THE COLOMBIAN ARMY

The Colombian Army traces its history back to the Army of the Commoners, the revolutionary army made up of peasants and other such militiamen during the days of the Colombian War of Independence. On July 20, 1810, Colombia declared its independence from Spanish Empire, following a long period of political instability within the Spanish Crown due to the Peninsula War. With the Spanish defeated temporarily, a period of nationwide instability and conflict known as the Foolish Fatherland broke out from 1810 to 1816. Between federalist and centralist, as many cities and provinces across the country set up their own autonomous juntas. Due to my country's challenged geography and the lack of communication between all the provinces and cities the juntas declared themselves sovereign from each other. This fragmentation prevents the proper development of the regular army, and would take nine years before a nation's army would be formed. During this time struggling with consolidation, the Spanish crown took full advantage and began a military campaign to reestablish the authority of the Spanish Empire. With the independence gained after the defeat of the Spanish Royalist forces at the battle of Boyacá in 1819 the Republic of Gran Colombia was established by the Constitution of Cucuta in 1821 with its capital in Bogota. There upon the Gran Colombian Army was formed.

THE COLOMBIA NATIONAL POLICE

I will be graduating next week. My parents were happy and proud, planning a celebration at a local cafe. On graduation day was a beautiful sunny day and all went well, and we headed to the cafe for our dinner celebration. The whole family was there and were waiting for us to arrive to surprise me.

I thought the dinner was just for me and my mother and father. When we entered the cafe, the whole place erupted in a loud Congratulation. I was so surprised and happy for my accomplishment. My father did not rent the entire cafe so many who didn't know any of us were offering their congratulations, even a small wedding party who rented the other hall next to ours. After things calmed down and everyone was seated, we heard what sounded like a car backfire and then more and then all hell broke loose—glass flying, people screaming and running. The noise was deafening so many guns firing into the hall next to ours. My family were running and diving on to the floor. When silence mercifully came, we discovered that two of my uncles were killed and three of my cousins were wounded; there was blood everywhere. The police said our family was hit and killed from stray bullets. We were not the target. The wedding party in the hall next to us killed everybody in the room: women, children, waiters, even the Catholic priest's blood was running out the door into the street. Body parts were everywhere. My mother and Father were crying sobbing. I was in tears. I went into the other hall and was sticking to the floor in the blood no one was alive just minutes ago twenty-five people were laughing and celebrating their future life. Why am I a trained medical person and can do nothing to help? All the studying for what good? Would being a doctor stop this from happening? I walked up to the front where the wedding party was sitting, and the wedding couple were holding hands heads on the table that was once white but now completely red with their blood both had their eyes open with a look I'll never forget. I started to leave and tripped over what I think was the bride's father; he was trying to get to her, and his head was almost blown off and so many wounds in his body. He was shot everywhere; one of the gunmen trained all of his effort on him and there was a gun by his side and a knife in his back with a message: You betray us we will kill all your family. The hall was now covered by national police; they were saying that the father was part of the national police, one of their officers working undercover in the cartel was discovered by what they believed was a corrupt politician. The commander said every time this happens, we lose more police we are afraid we don't know who to trust. We need more local young people to help. We are losing to the drug violence and the killing of our innocent people. My father found me and said for me to take my mother home and the rest of the family. I turned to him and I said, "I am going to do something to stop this, Father. Being a doctor is not enough. I am going to join the national police; I have to. I it owe to my family and these people who died for nothing." I found my mother with her family; they were loading my cousins into ambulances and my uncles were covered with white sheets lying on the floor. My mother was trying to console my aunts. They were hysterical; there was no way to calm them down; nothing she tried worked. They kept screaming why over and over again. I want to find and kill these animals that killed my uncles and hurt my cousins. After the funerals of my uncles and my cousins recovered in hospital, I told my mother of my plan to join the national police. At first, she said, "No you will not. I can't lose you too, we lost enough. You're going to help people as a doctor." I said being a doctor didn't help my uncles and all or those other people? I want to drive this out of our country, no more innocent people need to die or be hurt for drugs. Every time I close my eyes, I see the eyes of the bride and groom looking at me. I must do this.

TRAINING FOR THE NATIONAL POLICE

The first week of training was mostly paper-work, getting fitted for uniforms, and inter-views. With my experience, the commander was interested in talking to me directly which surprised me; this was not normal for him to talk to recruits. I was nervous when I was called into his office. When I walked into his office he stood and shook my hand and asked why a doctor wanted to join the police force. I thought about what I should say not to sound stupid or worse that I wanted revenge for my family. He said he was aware of what happened last year in the cafe and the loss of the lives and my family. He expressed his condolences. Then he asks, "Simon, are you here to get revenge for your family?" I said no I wanted to serve the people of Colombia. His reply sounded he-roic. "Are you a hero?" "No, I'm tired of in-nocent people getting killed and the country I love being destroyed." "Fine," he said, "let's see if you have what it takes. Over the next six weeks, we find out."

The second week was physical. The running miles were difficult for me. I've gotten out of shape sitting around since the incident last year at the cafe. My instructor said either I get in shape or I was going to wash out. I started running in the morning before sunup and before our morning physical training and late in the day after our day is over. It worked. I went from the back of the pack to the front, sometimes coming in first. The rest of the physical training was easy for me, so I excelled in gaining enough points to be the top recruit. My instructor was coming around and wasn't on me as much.

I was still running twice a day just to keep my advantage over the recruits. The last two weeks were weapons training and hand-to-hand combat areas I have no experience in. First time at the range I surprised myself by targeting ten bulls' eyes out of nineteen shots in my 9mm pistol. Considering I missed the first five shots completely not knowing what I was doing. My instructor gave me some instruction and ten out of fourteen was a good improvement. Considering my left eye, the

instructor was impressed. New weapon—
long gun training—same result with snipers'
weapons long gun, ten for ten, still top recruit. Final section hand-to-hand. I went to
my instructor. I was a little scared about
hand-to-hand combat. Fighting is something
I have no faith in my ability to accomplish
anything with this skill. I was correct in my
concern about this section of my training.
I was failing and had no success with and
matches against the other recruits. I was de-
pressed and was looking for any help I could
get and spent time working the heavy bag. As
I was getting my ass kicked by the heavy bag,
I heard a voice behind me. The voice turned
out to be the commander I spoke with five
weeks prior. He said he was following my
progress up to this point. He also said, "I am
aware of the trouble you are having. That is
why I am here to train you in martial arts to
get you to graduation and working for
Colombia." The training went on for two
weeks, long hours, and results that gave me
enough points to graduate in the top half of
the recruits' class. I lost my top spot which I
was angry about. I went to graduation by myself and nothing afterwards. I don't think I

will celebrate anything ever again. as I was leaving campus the command stopped me and asked if he could talk with me. I said sure and told him I owed him for his help. He told me he was taking over a special forces unit and he needed an operator who was a qualified medical professional so he thought of me as a doctor and a sniper in one would be a hell of an asset. I was interested and he told me to come back next week and report to the special force section of the campus.

SPECIAL FORCES ASSIGNMENT

On the day we gathered in a classroom, I looked at the twelve men in the room and one thing struck me as interesting. We all looked so much alike, all the same features. When the command walked in the room, we went silent and were intense and excited as to what this was about. He began saying we were a brand-new unit that was going undercover and infiltrating the cartels and the guerrillas to stop the killing in the streets. The plan was to come from Bogota so we would fit into the groups. We would try to be undercover in. My thoughts went to the cafe and what happened there to an undercover cop and his family and the loss of my uncles and my cousins. The training will be concentrated on drug cartels and all the guerilla groups so we would fit in. We study all their operations. We were instructed by drug task forces from different countries but mainly Colombia and the United States. The information went from Colombia to North America, and we spent six months in training. By the time it was over, all of us looked the part: long hair, beards, tattoos—whatever we needed to make sure we were not discovered. We were not allowed to leave or talk to anyone. In fact, the mother of one of my teammates died and he wasn't allowed to leave; we could trust no one.

EMBEDDED INTO GUERRILLAS

The Commander came to me at the gun range and said he thought he found a new cartel operating in Bogota. The rumor was they were working with the Mexican cartel. After the fall of the Medellin Cartel, the cities in Colombia were a war zone.

The plan was planting me into this cartel as an enforcer with a background established by the CIA of the United States drug task force with a rap sheet that would impress any career drug lord. The Commander handed over my credentials and weapon all provided by the CIA—untraceable. A meeting was set up by another cop operating as the CIA. A couple of weeks went by without any contact. I was on edge waiting, not easy. My new name was Carlos Rodriguez with my face and new tattoos. I certainly look the part. Can I sell myself as a killer, not sure. I know firsthand what these animals do to people and their family who betray them. I was just leaving my new apartment and a blacked-out SUV pulled up and the back doors flew open and two men jumped out, pointed a gun at me, and motioned for me to get in. Once in the back seat they put a sheet over my head a sped off. We drove for about half an hour making a series of left and right turns. I assumed to lose any tail that might be following the SUV. This made me very nervous because they are acting like they don't trust me, or they know who I really am. I might be headed to my death. The SUV came to a sliding stop, the back door flew open, and then I felt the two grab me and they pulled off the bag covering my head. I noticed we were at the waterfront and we were heading to a house on stilts over the water. All I could hear is screaming—loud, terrible screaming—as we walked up the ramp to the house something splashed into the water from under the house. The closer we got the smell was overwhelming, a smell that came right back to me: a distinct smell of blood and a lot of it. As we opened the door, we walked into a room with men women and children tied up sitting in chairs. There were six people—two men, three women, and one child—over in the corner was a man hanging from the ceiling by a rope; it looked like they cut the skin off his body, and he was alive and was begging to be killed. He was begging for them not to kill his family. The man standing in the room next to the trap door is a huge man. Just then the back door opened, and three men walked in, all carrying machetes. The room exploded in screams no and they grabbed the first man, knocked him down, and began chopping him—up his arms, legs, and finally his head. The man hanging from the rope was sobbing, "You killed my brother, you son of a bitch." They moved to the first women and repeated the process three times. I stood in shock again and witnessed the inhuman acts of the cartel. The little girl was crying and asking for her mother who she just watched be chopped up and dumped into the sea. I decided I was not going to let this little girl suffer her death in the hands of these animals. I drew my weapon and put a bullet in the head of the man hanging from the rope. Then I turned on the four others and shot all four in the head, killing all in the room. The two men who were waiting by the SUV stayed there. I untied the little girl and walked her out the door as I approached them. They were laughing, who were these assholes? The big guy spoke up and said, "They are from Mexico and we use them to keep people in line and afraid and to send fear to the people." I said, "Not anymore, they're all dead." "Dead? Who killed them?" "I did." They ask why and I said, "I am a killer but not this way; they didn't deserve this." "We heard five shots." "I killed the guy hanging by the rope. He cost the lives of his family; he certainly deserved to die."

The big guy said, "Let's get out of here." No bag over my head this time we drove back to my apartment and he told me and the little girl to get out. "We will be in touch when we need you. What are you going to do with her?" I said, "Not your concern. I'll take care of her." As we walked into my apartment, I looked for the throwaway phone given to me by the commander, an old flip phone—untraceable. I called and left a message and our code for a meeting ASAP. Everything I tried to calm her down was not working. She kept calling for her mother and her father. She screamed that I shot her father I had no explanation for her, telling her he was suffering and was going to die anyway and was responsible by his involvement with the cartel and trying to steal from them caused the death of his family. I was to meet the commander in the morning in the park and to bring the little girl with me and he would take care of her. The meeting was short and when the little girl left, I sat there and watched her walk away. I hoped she would have a better life. I somehow felt responsible for her and I did kill her father.

Two months and I heard nothing from the cartel. It was Friday night at 3 A.M. A knock on the door, I picked up my gun and went to the door, unlocking the bolt but left the heavy chain that I installed for moments just like this. I pointed my weapon at the guy right in front of the chain. I recognized the same big guy who came the last time. When he saw the gun, he said, "Any way to greet a friend? Are you going to let me in?" I unlatch the chain and open the door. "I have a job for you. Are you interested?" "Well, what is it?" "What do you think is your specialty?" He gave me the details and the time and the place. Nothing else other than a photo, and I am supposed to kill this guy at the park on Sunday at noon. The photo is of an older man tall with a beard all gray looks like a lawyer or a businessman. The big guy was gone as quick as he came. I needed to know who this man is. I get my throwaway and called the commander and advised him of the hit. He asks me to meet to show the photo, so we planned a meeting at a bar the police use to meet informants. When I showed him the photo, he knew him. The commander said he was a crooked politician and the police expected him in giving cartels information about Cis, undercover police, judges, and other politicians. I ask why the cartel would want him dead. Probably knows too much— a liability. I said, "What should I do?" The commander said, "Carry out the hit." "Why would you want me to kill this man?" "We need you undercover in the cartel you are in and could bring down this cartel along with contacts to the Mexican Cartel. You have your orders at the end of discussion." Sunday, I got up early, went to the street across from the park and went into the building and was able to get to the roof. The sniper nest was the perfect line of sight I set up and just had to wait. My target arrived right on time and sat where I was told he would be by himself. Lining up my shot, I took a breath slowly and let it pull the trigger. He slumped down on the bench with the top of his head gone. Weeks turned into months, the hits continued, and every time I would meet the commander to get the police sanction for the killings. It seemed I was targeting revival Colombian guerrilla group leaders. When I met with my commander, he said I was reducing the drug traffic and stopping the killing of innocent Colombians and I was okay with that. My only concern was my group is now all Mexican targeting and eliminating all their competition. It's been a week since my last hit and I thought maybe it was done, no targets left. My official kills were fifteen including the five in the house saving the little girl I never saw again. I received another visit from my late-night visitor with another hit. I asked who this was. He said, "A cop we had on our payroll refused additional information regarding the task force operating in Colombia. They are having success. We had to change our route to North America from the Caribbean Islands through Mexico. This is costing millions of dollars and 30 percent of the drugs because Mexicans want to be paid with drugs. The time and place were tomorrow in front of the courthouse where the official will be at a press conference about the task force." When he left, I opened the file and was shocked that the official was the local chief of police who I knew before I was a cop. I reached out to the commander and advised who my target was and told him the backstory for the hit. The commander was quiet for a long time and looked at me. I ask him to bring me in, that I didn't or couldn't do this, he is a cop and has been for many years; this could not be true. The commander broke silence and said, "It all true. We have known for years he is an informant for the cartels and have taken money for his betrayal. He deserves to pay for his sins; you must continue the hit." I objected and told him my fear that they were using me to get rid of their competition;

this group is getting more powerful. I again asked to come in out of hiding; he denied my request and gave the sanction for the hit. This hit would be difficult to get close. He claimed he would make it possible to get access to the building across the street with the line of sight from the bell tower at the top of the building. A bright sunny Monday morning, the press conference started right on time and my target was right where he was supposed to be. When he began to speak, I put a bullet right between his eyes. Blood splattered over everyone at the podium number 16 and he was dead. I backed up and left. The commander made sure of my escape just like he said he would. When I arrived back to my apartment the big guy was waiting in my apartment with two new guys I never seen before. Then the door opened and a younger Mexican man dressed in an expensive suit walked in with two more big guys. He didn't introduce himself. No names were exchanged. He handed me an envelope sealed and said, "Open this when we leave not before," and thanked me for my dedication. As fast as they came, they left. It was filled with a lot of money. Soon as they left, I called the commander and requested a meeting for tonight. I didn't say anything about the money; I took the envelope to a safe deposit box I keep for my personal items. We were to meet at the cafe down the street from my apartment. I was going to tell the commander I needed to quit, and I couldn't kill anymore. I would return to my family and be the doctor they wanted. As I rounded the corner, I saw an SUV parked in front of the café, and two men were standing outside the SUV. As I approached the SUV the rear window opened, and the commander spoke to me. I was surprised, I never saw the two other men approach. The commander said he was sorry then I felt pressure at the back of my neck, I saw a light and Twelve figures chanting THE CURSE OF THE RED ROSE. I see a shield of gold and red. Simon dies from having his throat cut.

CHAPTER THIRTEEN

CIVIL WAR AND THE ROLE OF BLACK SOLDIERS

The American Civil War was the defining event in our nation's history. Between 1861 and 1865 10,000 battles and engagements were fought across the continent, from Vermont to the New Mexico Territory, and beyond. Many elements of civil scholarship are still hotly debated. One is the role of Black soldiers who fought for the Union. With the issuance of the Emancipation Proclamation in September 1862, African Americans—both free and runaway slaves—came forward to volunteer for the Union and caused substantial numbers. Beginning in October, approximately 180,000 African-Americans, comprising 163 units, served in the U.S. Army, and 18,000 in the Navy. That month, the 1st Kansas Colored Volunteers repulsed a Confederate attack at Island Mount, Missouri. Men of the U.S.C.T. (United States Colored Troops) units went on to distinguish themselves on the battlefields east and west. Random public assaults on men of color in uniform, violence toward Blacks in northern cities, and mistreatment by white comrades and the enemy afflicted on the Blacks' troops. The fact that Black soldiers were paid less was a particularly offensive issue; Black enlisted men and officers received only seven dollars per month whereas white privates earned thirteen dollars. Due to the intervention and protest of Frederick Douglass, The Governor of Massachusetts and commanding officers such as Col. Higginson and Col. Robert Gould Shaw, the unequal pay issue was amended by mid-1864. in spite of the injustices, the Colored Troops demonstrated their determination and bravery in a number of engagements in the final two years of the war.

The earliest major offensives in which Black troops participated were in Louisiana, at Port Hudson and Milliken's Bend, in May and June of 1863. By far, however, the most famous was the assault on Fort Wagner at Charleston, South Carolina by the 54th Massachusetts Infantry. John A. Andrew, Massachusetts' influential abolitionist governor, directed the organization of this distinctive unit, the first Black regiment of the North. Col. Robert Gould Shaw and Lt. Edward N. Hallowell, two young Northern men with anti-slavery and humanitarian backgrounds, were chosen to lead the proud men of the 54th. Shaw had studied at Harvard and in Europe, and served at Antietam before accepting command of the Black unit. In May 1863, with great confidence and high expectations, Col. Shaw's regiment departed Boston for the South in a jubilant parade attended by many dignitaries and well-wishers. A few days later, Shaw reflected, "if the raising of colored troops proves such a benefit to the country and to the blacks... I shall thank god a thousand times that I was led to take my share in it." Once in South Carolina, Shaw pressed for his anxious men to take part in the operations against Charleston's fortifications. The opportunity presented itself on July 18, 1863 when some 600 tired and starving, but anxious men of the 54th led the charge against

Fort Wagner on Morris Island outnumbered by a larger Confederate force inside the fort. The 54th suffered many losses including the twenty-five-year-old Shaw.

My name is Alexander H. Pickett "Patch" and I am named after the Plantation Owner. I'm a slave on a cotton and tobacco Plantation in South Carolina. I work in the fields with planting and picking the crops and taking care of the animals. I've worked for Mr. Pickett since I was a boy and he treats me well. My wife Porsha is Mr. Pickett's house slave and she helps her mother Mama Sally as the Pickett's house maid and cook. Mama Sally has always looked after me. My mother died in childbirth. I don't know my father. I was born with no left eye, just a hole where my eye should be and a huge scar on my forehead. Mama Sally made me a patch to cover the hole where my eye should be. The life of a slave offered little hope and no freedom other than your little time you get at the end of the day. Master Pickett was kind to us maybe because of Mama Sally and he felt sorry for me. Mama Sally believed that Master Pickett was my father. She was sure; she and my mother were close, and my mother worked in the house and my mother was the upstairs maid and was a beautiful young woman. He had many opportunities to be with her. Mama Sally is convinced; me, I'm not so sure. Master Pickett is concerned about the war. A lot of the Plantations in the area are falling to the north and being over-run. The slaves a lot of them are joining the Union army to fight for freedom. I spoke to Mama Sally and my wife Porsha and told them if the Union troops overran our plantation, I would join the Union army. Mama Sally and Porsha were concerned and afraid and said nothing more. The next morning Master Pickett summoned me to his office and told me he was going to send me to the confederate army to serve in his place as his slave. When I ask when he said in the next couple of weeks. He promised to take care of Porsha and Mama Sally. I left his office without saying a thing. After talking to Porsha and Mama Sally I decided not to wait for the Union Army. I would run away to join the Union Army and take them with me. We plan on leaving in the next couple of days. Mama Sally told Porsha she would stay at the plantation. She was too old to change her life now but wanted Porsha to go and be free. We left before sunup and headed for the war. It was not hard to find; it was all around us. At midday we ran straight into the 54th Union Army. At gunpoint we told them we wanted to join the army to fight for our freedom. We were taken to an officer and were told we could join the 54th and would begin the process. After training Porsha and I were members of the 54th—her as nurse and me as a soldier. Our service begins. The 54th Massachusetts was one of the Black regiments who fought for the Union in the Civil War. The 54th started recruiting in February 1863 and trained at Camp Meigs on the outskirts of Boston, Massachusetts. Prominent abolitionists were active in the recruitment efforts, including Fredrick Douglas whose sons were the first to enlist. Black soldiers proved their mettle and ability. July 18, 1863, the 54th Massachusetts Infantry led the assault on Fort Wagner. The fort was a stronghold for the Confederate Army, heavily fortified by artillery. Against heavy artillery and rifle fire we charged into the fort, engaging in hand-to-hand combat. We were taking heavy casualties, our advance was repelled, and we retreated but we fought with a passion and determination that changed minds on how Black soldiers would honor the

Union in the War against the South. We lost
half of our troops including our Colonel, a
twenty-five-year-old white officer who would
be buried with his troops. My beloved Porsha
was shot trying to help a wounded soldier.
The fighting was nothing like the training. It
was horrible, death and bodies everywhere,
young men screaming for their mothers, calling on help from God. There were pools of
blood everywhere. How and why was I still
alive? We heard that two weeks later the
Confederate troops evacuated Fort Wagner,
and I took some peace knowing that the lives
lost were not in vain. We accomplished a
blow for Black troops and the North with
fighting for no pay because of the 54th boy-
cott for earning less than our white comrades.
There are rumors among the officers that it
was going to change. I received a field pro-
motion to sergeant. After marching 120 miles
in 102 hours to cover the Union retreat at the
Battle of Olustee, we lost eighty-six men in
the battle. I with a small group of men was
ordered to Fort Pillow, and we would leave
for Memphis in the morning. It took thirty-
one days for the march. Once we arrived, we
reported to the commander. After a week of
leave, assigned patrol outside the fort on

patrol, we came upon an advancing Confederate. We ran back hard to the fort to report the advance. The Confederates including sharpshooters open a barrage of bullets down on the fort killing our commander. The Confederate General demanded unconditional surrender. Outnumbered by the enemy, our second in command now assumed command and refused to surrender. The Confederates renewed the attack and overran the fort and drove us down toward the river bluff into a deadly crossfire. Our lines broke and many of our troops threw down their muskets and rushed down the bluff toward the river. The rebels kept firing on, murderously killing unarmed surrendering soldiers. Many of the Black soldiers seeing there was no quarter to be given jumped into the river while the rebels stood on the banks and on the bluff shooting us in the head. Bullets were striking water around our heads, and the muddy river suddenly turned red with the blood of Black Union soldiers. As I lie there, I feel a terrible pain and then nothing another pain in my chest I see a group of soldiers and a bright light with a gold shield. They chant THE CURSE OF THE RED ROSE.

EPILOGUE

The curse of the rose still travels through time. Souls destined to find closure and peace. Discover the battles, the wars, the horrible deaths that plague the human race. Will the curse end? Only when mankind stops killing each other or will peace find them and let their souls rest. The answer is in a future chapter in a soon to be released sequel of A SOLDIER'S HELL.

Dick THERESA
THANKS FOR the
INTREST
ENJOY
MY FIRST BOOK
James Flaherty
" A SOLDIERIS HELL